A Caddo's Way

A Caddo's Way

Jeffrey DeLotto

LITERARY PRESS
LAMAR UNIVERSITY

ISBN: 978-1-942956-58-7
Library of Congress Control Number: 2018959633

Lamar University Literary Press
Beaumont, Texas

For Jack Mitchell, a Texas ranger and hunter,
and his uncle, Francois Michel, a French-Indian trader,
for passing some Caddo stories down that first hooked me.

Other books by Jeffrey DeLotto

8 Voices: Contemporary Poetry of the American Southwest
Days of a Chameleon, Collected Poems
Voices at the Door
Voices Writ in Sand: Dramatic Monologues and Other Poems

Other fiction from Lamar University Literary Press

Robert Bonazzi, *Awakened by Surprise*
David Bowles, *Border Lore: Folktales and Legends of South Texas*
Chris Carmona, Rob Johnson & Chuck Taylor, *The Beatest State in the Union*
Kevin K. Casey, *Four-Peace*
Terry Dalrymple, *Love Stories (Sort Of)*
Gerald Duff, *Memphis Mojo*
Britt Haraway, *Early Men*
Michael Howarth, *Fair Weather Ninjas*
Gretchen Johnson, *The Joy of Deception*
Christopher Linforth, *When You Find Us We Will Be Gone*
Tom Mack & Andrew Geyer, *A Shared Voice*
Moumin Quazi, *Migratory Words*
Harold Raley, *Lost River Anthology*
Harold Raley, *Louisiana Rouge*
Jim Sanderson, *Trashy Behavior*
Jan Seale, *Appearances*
Melvin Sterne, *The Number You Have Reached*
Melvin Sterne, *The Shoeshine Boy*
John Wegner, *Love Is Not a Dirty Word*
Robert Wexelblatt, *The Artist Wears Rough Clothing*

Chapter 1

The purposeful mile-eating trot of several horses snapped Two Hawks to attention, and he stepped into the shadow of a large sycamore at the road's verge and slid to the ground in the leaning squat of an idle wayfarer, sliding his eyes toward the road as four determined riders made their way south toward Natchitoches with more resolve than he wished to encounter.

One rider, his whispy blond beard blown back, stood in his stirrups and spat to the side, barely missing Two Hawks where he sat oblivious to this young man's attention. The old Caddo waited until their dull hoofbeats on the packed clay road had been absorbed by the moisture-laden air of the early morning.

Natchitoches—1824, they called it, though the number meant nothing to him. However, the indelible image of his last visit not many seasons past was sharp as flame before his eyes, the soft resistance of the collapsed flesh of the Caddo woman's abdomen as he had withdrawn the hand's length of knife blade, his knife, as she slumped forward in seated death.

He had wiped the blade on her doeskin skirt moments before two young soldiers broke open the storehouse and found him. His had been an ignominious exit into the thicket after a flintlock's misfire.

But a short time ago, Two Hawks had felt a strong tug, like the pull of a heavy catfish on the line, drawing him toward the settlement, the hollow feeling of something left undone, unfinished, though he didn't know what it might be. Something Dr. Sibley had said to him, though, during his last stay, came back to him as it had many times since.

In the doctor's study, picking at a bowl of sugared and toasted pecans, the men had worked their way through a second rum toddy in a desultory fashion, unrolling years like cured tobacco leaves, when after a long silence mostly old men and ancient couples can be comfortable with, Sibley spoke: "Inevitable solitude is the terror of consciousness, and its sole respite."

The doctor sometimes made such profound and often incomprehensible pronouncements, and Two Hawks had waited patiently with a questioning eye until a forthcoming explanation allowed the Caddo to put the words to use, and he had been reminded why he sought the doctor's company on occasion, in small doses. He grunted assent, and they had looked into each other's minds with a kinship bound with hoops of steel. On this journey the doctor would have something to say, were he still above ground, which called to mind an earlier encounter this morning.

The slow, methodical scrape of small claws had awakened him, his eyelids snapping open in the early spring dawn, and he had blinked twice slowly but otherwise did not move until he had identified the intrusion. Not two paces away, beneath the early dewberry vines, a tortoise, orange-flecked to mirror the broken sunlight that shafted through the branches, worked first her forelegs and then the hind, like clawed paddles biting into the surface of the forest floor leaves.

Two Hawks had smiled slowly, he recalled, at this energy to make new life, knew the female was scooping out a soft nest to deposit her eggs, creating the next generation, when the sharp click of an iron horseshoe upon stone had caused both early risers to remain still.

The lone horseman on the Camino Real had paced his mount at a walk, and the box turtle resumed her task, but the sound of her nails in soil changed as her forelegs sought purchase on a smooth surface with a sound more hollow than stone, more smooth than wood.

The old Caddo had raised himself on one elbow, spilling off the loose leaves he habitually covered himself with each night, to draw less attention to his sleeping form.

The mother tortoise, they all looked ancient though in fact she may have been a few hands of seasons old, dug forward, scraped hollowly and fell back, with little result, repeatedly, until Two Hawks pushed himself up onto his knees and leaned over, peering into the shallow pit that had been swept smoothly out under the leaf floor, his breath catching and slowly released.

Swept clean at the bottom of the intended nest, the dull soiled white of bone rounded up through the detritus like a buried stone. Bending forward, he had pushed the female terrapin aside, she, finding her prospective nest disturbed, trundled further under the brush to find a more secluded spot.

Running his crooked fingers over the exposed dome, Two Hawks

8

had gently probed the cracked surface and brushed away the damp leaves of several seasons, a not unpleasant realization coming over his thoughts as muted tribal designs showed the unearthed dome to be the bottom of a clay pot instead of the skull he had at first thought.

"Still a grave of sorts," he had said aloud to the old water oak bearded with gray moss under whose heavy limbs he sat. He had thought of the busy Caddo village that had long ago thrived among their beehive dwellings, how they would have recently planted the spring's three sisters in each stick-punched hole, the corn and bean and squash seeds resting together as if in conspired conversation.

First the corn would sprout and begin its green thrusting sensuously toward the sun, soon to provide the support needed by the tendrils of sprouted beans. Finally, the wide spreading leaves of the squash plant would shade the bases of all three plants and help to hold the precious moisture needed to bring forth the bounty.

Such balance had there been, but for the occasional Osage encroachment or thieving sweep of fever's heavy hand, though even in those some satisfaction had been found.

A moment more he had sat, in this very midst of spring, sat so still to hear the very growth, the crisp new leaves like infants' ears breaking through the green skin of new buds.

Chapter 2

Two Hawks snorted a chuckle to himself as he neared the outlying sheds of the growing settlement: his heart felt almost a leap, as when a rabbit spooked from a trailside clump of grass where it should have known better than to take refuge. He knew that at any moment he might look up to see Margaret Hays, now known as Madame Dupre, though she had never married the town's military commander. He also was concerned that even though more than two hands of years had passed since he had recovered his knife from the bowels of She-de-a, the whites often had long memories about what they considered to be "serious crimes." The two young soldiers, now mature men, still may recognize him ...

And he looked further back through the mist of years to where he had first encountered the woman's crime, to the matter of the Hanasai ear spool. Two Hawks had squatted in the sun of the clearing, the feathery branches of cypress soughing in the faint summer breeze. He had glanced around at this palm of land at the end of a swampy arm near Sod'ha Lake, the fingers of cypress roots reaching up out of the mud and tepid water, holding him secure here, smoke rising from the morning fire, carried off into the brightening sky.

"I must go south again," he remembered he had said aloud, only a nearby crow cocking his blue-black head to listen. "How simple for you," Two Hawks said to the bird's bright yellow eye. "But look at these things here and tell me what they mean."

Unlike other Caddo, Two Hawks had neither farm nor family, both lost many seasons of wandering ago, as he sought to understand and could not remain still.

The yellow flames had licked up the sides of his smoke-blackened copper bowl, the tin lining shining like a mussel shell as the water broke into a rolling boil. The old man opened a pouch at his waist and took out a flat brown block imprinted with the French coat of arms that he had acquired at the trading post near the abandoned Fort St. John Baptiste. With his heavy steel knife he shaved off two bark-like pieces of the compressed tea and dropped them carefully into the water, watching it gradually turn reddish-brown and fill the air with its aroma.

Up on the raised bank nearby a rattling in the leaves beneath a magnolia tree drew Two Hawks' eye, and the beaded shell of an armadillo burrowed into a patch of sunlight, stopped, snuffed at some inhaled mold, and moved on.

The magnolia buds had swayed rhythmically in the breeze, would at summer's end look like the soft-cupped hands of dancers calling for the fall rain, bringing to the old man's mind the story his mother had told, of how the blossoms had come to be ...

Two Hawks had later mused, creasing his eyes in self-indulgence at his own dependence on outsiders, rinsing the tea and Spanish sugar residue from his bowl after relishing his morning tea. The dry snap of a tupelo branch ringing out in the still air stopped his hand for just a moment travelling toward the pouch at his back. His eyes slid to his right, now his head following as the figure of a young Caddo with the tattoos and beaded breechclout of the Yatasi stepped carelessly through the underbrush, obviously causing noise as a warning of his approach. Two

Hawks had already followed the man's movements for some time but pretended surprise as the latter stepped forward and spoke:

"Hanistih, Old One, I did not mean to scare you. Are you the one called Two Hawks?"

The older Caddo looked into the distance. "His shadow sits beside me."

Confused for a moment, the messenger continued, watching uneasily as the fading black tattoos of birds' talons seemed to move up and down the man's shining arms while he tied his beaded pouches. "Bintah, Xinesi of the Sod'ha Yatasi, asks Two Hawks to—" the old man looked up, seeming to challenge the messenger's power— "to the village. His son has been killed, found ... alone. He said you would know."

"I will come," said Two Hawks, after a pause.

"Will you come with me now? I was told to bring you ..."

"Tell him I will come," Two Hawks said, and stared into the fire's embers as the man finally moved away.

The main village of the Yatasi, an independent tribe within the Natchitoches Confederacy north along the Red River near the Great Raft, had crowded one end of a rich savannah with the traditional Caddo beehive lodges rising in tight golden cones, the late morning smoke from fires drifting from their peaks in lazy feathers.

Wondering why the village dogs had not barked, one woman, seated before a stretched deerskin, her red and purple-painted breasts swinging from side to side as she rubbed brains into a lustrous black hide, paused in her work as Two Hawks approached.

Following the old ways of greeting by weeping, Two Hawks' eyes filled with tears as he said, "Tell me, Nutitsi, star of the day, where is the lodge of the Xinesi, Bintah?"

Younger, disconcerted by his display of emotion, she indicated a larger grass lodge across the clearing, and went back to the hide frame, secretly smiling at his compliment.

Bending low to exit the doorway that was the lodge's only opening other than the smoke hole, Bintah straightened to find Two Hawks standing, waiting, some ten paces away. Both elder men wept quietly in greeting before seating themselves in the shade of the lodge. The warm smell of the sun-baked straw always reminded Two Hawks of his childhood, and of happier days spent with ...

"Hanistih, Two Hawks," the spiritual leader said. "Red Bear, my sister's child, told us last night he had heard you were passing near. I am fortunate to find you—perhaps it is the spirit of iwi. I heard long ago how you sometimes learn the thoughts of those who died."

"Sometimes, Bintah," the other corrected. "I come to learn what has been hidden in the thoughts of the living."

"Help me, Hanistih. There is talk that my oldest son, Nao'tsi, has cast aside his own life, and the signs point that way. This cannot be. I am not just a blind old a'a—that cannot be."

Two Hawks looked into the eyes of the old leader, saw more than sadness there, and said, "May I look upon your son that is gone?"

Chapter 3

At the back of the i'ne's lodge, the body had been wrapped in a thick, soft black bearskin in preparation for burial. Slowly, with care and respect, the visiting Caddo laid the folds of the pelt back to expose the man, a well-muscled mature gao-can, or brave.

Two Hawks was alone with Bintah. The village leader began: "My son was found yesterday afternoon a short walk south near the trace to the salt works. Several had heard the shot earlier, but when he did not return, Tanaha, his du wi, younger brother, went looking. Nao'tsi was found under a large pecan tree, his musket next to him. Tanaha said his brother's moccasin was off, his toe in the guard ..."

"I understand, old father," Two Hawks said. "I have heard of such things."

Bintah continued: "A trader stopping with us told us he had found a French trapper last spring that way—"

"When was this?"

"Last full moon, at the night of the Turkey Dance."

"Will you permit me to be with your son alone so that we may speak in private?"

The body had begun to swell in the warmth of midsummer, so with difficulty Two Hawks removed first one moccasin and then the other, noting with a grunt the largest toe on the right foot revealed dried blood and a small cut as from a trigger guard, though in other respects the toe appeared normal, as did the others. He also noted an ear spool, like one Two Hawks had once seen from a robbed Caddo mound of the Old People, two fingers wide, copper-sheathed siltstone, wired through the left ear. The other ear had only a long hole.

The man's face still showed the shock of death, powder burns and black spots of impregnated unburned powder clear on his painted cheeks. Two Hawks noted one broken front tooth, a tiny smear of lead on the edge where the musket ball had passed on its way toward the roof of the man's mouth. The bullet clearly was still lodged in the skull.

There were no other signs or marks on the body. Swollen but shining with bear grease, the arms and legs were artfully covered in deep black tattoos of claw marks of the bear and jagged lightning strikes, unlike Two Hawks' tattoos lovingly incised by his wife and aging father so long ago, the ash now fading. He replaced the covering over the body and began to compose many questions. Others had been answered.

Bintah then showed Two Hawks the son's musket, a typical smooth-bore .69 caliber flintlock trade gun of French manufacture; the father explained that his son had acquired the piece two moon cycles previously, and Two Hawks turned the weapon over in his hands, noting the polished stock now carefully inlaid with freshwater clamshell and copper studs, the brass patch box stuffed with greased cotton circles in which to wrap the lead balls before they were rammed home down the arm's-length browned barrel. The gun was obviously cherished and well cared for.

The copper powder flask with self-measuring spout and the black leather shot pouch were also examined, as was his heavy steel knife not unlike Two Hawks' own. Bintah wondered at the other man's interest in these items but said nothing, except to say that these things, having considerable power, would in this instance be passed down to the man's unborn son, rather than buried with him.

Accompanied by the younger brother, Two Hawks was then taken back to where the dead man had been found, passing as they did the quietly moaning widow rocking back and forth outside the lodge. He attempted to calm the young man, Tanaha, explaining that the place of death might need to be put to rest, the spirits of the woods often confused by a death without balance or meaning, but the other son was obviously unallayed.

The ancient pecan tree, its branches heavy with growing nut pods, towered over the surrounding hackberries and sweetgums, the grass and dewberry thickets thinning as the two men neared the massive trunk as thick as the height of a man, dead leaves and rotting branches deep near the base. A disturbed area three strides across was indicated by the younger brother as the place where the body was found, gathered up, and carried back to the village.

"Again, have patience with an old man," Two Hawks said. "Return to your lodge. I wish to speak to the Haiyoshatsi, the magic little people, of this place and will return soon."

"There is nothing for you here, hanistih. He is gone!" Angry, the second son tightened his grip on his rifle, ignoring the sign of the amayxoya on the right shoulder of the old brave. "My father understood nothing. Go from this place. These are not your people!"

"Indeed, after so many years, all the dead are my people. Among the living I am a stranger. Please, son, go back. I will not trouble the spirit of your ine."

Tanaha turned angrily away, leaving Two Hawks deep in thought watching his glistening back recede through the nearby hardwood thicket. The old Caddo then squatted beneath the tree and glanced around the disturbed area, plucking up a shred of cotton, replacing several overturned patches of leaves, under one of which a busy cluster of red ants was brushed off several smoked catfish bones and what after a taste turned out to be a small crust of sweetened corn cake. Further searches and rearrangements caused only disappointment, in part by what he had *not* found.

He then rose, hobbled about until the stiff joints ceased clouding his vision, and began a slow widening circle around the tree, closely watching the ground—and at last finding the sign he knew must be there.

Later, a group of tishiyatsis, boys of about ten suns, were teasing a bow-length kohuh, an alligator, its hind leg tethered to a peg driven into the ground at the edge of the clearing as Two Hawks stepped into the fading sunlight near Bintah's lodge.

He spoke quietly to the seated old priest: "You have seen clearly, Xinesi. Your son's life was taken by another. If you wish the truth, do as I ask. I will not say you wish to know."

The evening meal was brought to the low benches in front of

14

Bintah's lodge, beginning with woven grass mats laden with thick slices of melons heavy and moist from the recent rain. Seated around the clearing were Bintah, his feet resting on the traditional Xinesi stool, and Tasha Shahat, the village Caddi, or civil ruler, at the head of the oblong facing west, next to whom sat Tanaha on the north and Two Hawks on the right.

After overseeing the order of food presentation, the women took their seats: T'ao, the in'a, or mother, of Nao'tsi and Tanaha, wife of Bintah; and She-de-a, wife of the dead Nao'tsi, the grieving woman noted earlier, obviously very warm in the full deerskin shift but perhaps feeling the need for modesty and reserve. However, Two Hawks could still not quickly pass over her striking beauty, the long, thick hair and wet, heavy lashes. Nor could the loose deerskin entirely conceal her heavy breasts and swollen belly.

Bintah deferred to Tasha Shahat, who took the stone pipe, lit the powdered tobacco, and then offered blown smoke to the sky and the four directions, before sending the pipe around in order of age.

Following the melons, individual reed plates of roasted venison backstrap and liver were brought, accompanied by smoked fish and corn cakes sweetened with molasses and crisp green peppers.

After some time, while discussions of trading experiences and tribal disputes were passed in a desultory manner, polished pottery bowls of prairie chicken stewed with onion and sage were passed around. And perhaps Two Hawks was thought rude by some as he twice asked She-de-a to pass him the bowl of chicken for more. But at last all were finished and sat back to enjoy bowls of fragrant sassafras broth.

"So," Tanaha said, "Two Hawks, hanistih of a lost tribe, you have asked us to join you—and I assume you wish to tell us you are satisfied?"

"I am satisfied—"

"Well, then—"

"I am satisfied," Two Hawks began again, "that your brother did not take his own life."

"Then a mistake?" the Caddi offered.

"There was no mistake. He was killed."

"That cannot be true. Who would do this thing? For what reason?" asked T'ao.

"There is always a reason. Who would benefit from his death?" Two Hawks asked.

"I would!" Tanaha shot back quickly. "Only I. I would then be next in line one day to become Xinesi. But he shot himself—I found him with his toe ... What makes you think something else happened?"

Two Hawks looked at each person in turn and began: "I have encountered before men who have taken their own lives. There are always signs, moods, solitudes, a carelessness toward the objects of this world. But when the opportunity is presented, the man usually is convinced—the will must be there. I saw none of this. And forgive me if I speak in detail of the dead, but the body of Nao'tsi told me much."

"Who killed him, then?" Bintah demanded.

"The body did not tell me. But the pattern of powder burns on the face suggested that the muzzle of the rifle had been close, very close, but *outside* of his mouth when the weapon was fired, confirmed by the trace of lead from the musket ball on his broken tooth. Upon examining the man's feet, I discovered that indeed his right big toe did have a cut across it from the trigger guard, as it might from the kickback of the fired rifle. But here I must tell you that something worried me: there should have been bruising on the toe from a recoil like that, and there was none. I was seeing the work of a thinking killer, someone who had put the dead man's toe into the trigger guard and cut it *after* the shot was fired—"

"But we cannot believe that," said T'ao.

"Permit me to continue. I was disturbed, though, by what I did not find. The place where the body was found told me more: a shred of burned cotton patch expelled from the muzzle was caught under a cluster of creeper and confirmed that the shot had been fired outside the man's mouth; otherwise, the patch would have been in the mouth. A man intent upon taking his own life does not take that kind of chance but puts the muzzle firmly between his teeth—"

"That's enough!" cried She-de-a. "I cannot hear any more."

"Wife of Nao'tsi, whose child do you carry?" Two Hawks suddenly said.

Tanaha jumped to his feet. "My child! I do not know what magic you have used or what the spirits have told you, but leave her alone. I killed him—I killed my brother. He never understood She-de-a, never wanted to give her what she needed ... Do with me what you will."

Bintah rose, trembling as rage and sorrow warred across his frame. "I know nothing of my children. What have I grown?"

16

Two Hawks, still seated, spoke: "No, Tanaha, you are a noble young man and have perhaps gathered thoughts, but you did not kill your brother. The pecan tree told a different story. Please be seated. I found among the leaves the remains of a delicious snack—did you bring him a midday meal, Tanaha? You cannot tell me what you brought. And where is the ear spool that was in his left ear? Only one other person here can tell us that—the same person whose tracks I found approaching the tree and leaving it from the south, the person who lovingly brought his food and asked him in apparent innocence how a man might kill himself as the trader suggested, the same person who knelt down and jokingly but firmly pulled the trigger ... Pass me some more broth, please, She-de-a, and show us your thumb ..."

Chapter 4

In this part of the Louisiana Territory, the choice of long gun had been basically narrowed to three. The dominant weapon to the north was the Brown Bess, the British Land Pattern musket that had by this time been produced in three variations, primarily differing in overall length from sixty-two to forty-two inches, all models in .75 caliber (3/4 inch).

The other two options were the French Charleville .69 caliber musket with a thirty-two inch barrel and an American Springfield version of the same design produced at Harper's Ferry, also in .69 caliber.

Two Hawks had been given a Charleville .69 caliber musket, not new but worn in careful use, by Dr. John Sibley, who a number of years ago had been very grateful for the Caddo's knowledge of local herbs and his untiring help during a dysentery outbreak at Natchitoches in 1804. Cognizant of suspicions among many whites, the doctor had brought the rifle to the local blacksmith, who carefully engraved "gift presented to Caddo Two Hawks, by Dr. John Sibley, April 1804," to reassure his friend that other whites would readily identify the weapon's owner.

The Caddo also appreciated the idea that the .69 caliber ball was easily available in other parts of the territory, fitting both the French and American models. He cherished the musket, having decorated the buttstock with a series of brass studs in the lightning bolt design denoting swift power to the Caddoes. Three long groves were cut along the forestock, denoting the talons of his namesake.

Rather than the paper ball and powder cartridge favored by a growing number of soldiers and frontiersmen, Two Hawks had still preferred a small leather ball pouch, with the accompanying powder horn and measuring funnel, perhaps not as fast as the progressive paper cartridge but better suited in the southern territory for keeping moisture away from the powder.

Or at least this arrangement had worked for the old Caddo until the spring of 1825, when he once again made his way along the old Camino Real to Natchitoches, having witnessed firsthand the effectiveness of the new percussion capped rifles and more than a few conversions of the old flintlock models. He told himself that his purpose in coming this way was to see if his old friend, Samuel Corey, a blacksmith he had spent many hours with over the years as the man had made repairs to the Indian's rifle or fashioned a new point of haft on his old trade knife (the latter being close to three fingers shorter than when it was new), was still walking the land of the flesh.

Best not to have what someone else wanted, Two Hawks said to himself, as he often did, as a farm wagon rattled past on the road leading into Natchitoches, but a horse would have spared his old bones some walking ... He kept his head down, knowing a horse or a pair of eyes were remarkable, a humble old Caddo almost invisible.

And this is what they call 1825, though he saw this as another of the settlers' almost unslakable desire to count, to enumerate things, cows, bags of corn, money, years, as if 1850 would matter to his gnawed bones, scattered, he had no doubt, off some isolated trail.

Natchitoches just kept growing, the sounds and scents of activity swelling out like a rolling wave as the older log buildings, even out this far, had been overtaken by lumbered homes with filigreed porches, homespun increasingly relegated to the barns or tobacco sheds, and a gaggle of older women rustled past, their full skirts held just high enough to clear the red hardened clay of the roadway, bonnets wagging, pausing briefly in their conversation to whisper together in hushed tones, about the sad old Indian probably coming to town to buy a few tobacco twists with some beadwork or rolled deerskins. He was pleased with their dismissal.

Although Natchitoches and its immediate environs to the east had been under firm control for some time, with the Red River serving as a reliable transportation thoroughfare for points south, the Great Raft restricting water travel to the north, Two Hawks was coming in from the west, a considerable patch of which crawled with the lawless. Having changed nationality several times in the preceding fifty years, the area known as "Neutral Ground" or "No Man's Land in Louisiana" was a vast forested and swampy strip where a variety of would-be colonists, traders, renegades and runaways, outlaws and deserters had operated with no established law for many years.

After several aborted attempts to agree on the boundary between Louisiana and what would one day become Texas, the latter an important part of New Spain, negotiations had ceased when Spain severed diplomatic relations with the United States in 1805. As a result, conflicts and skirmishes both spoken and between troops broke out on both sides of the Sabine River.

Since neither country had wanted extended hostilities, Spanish Lt. Colonel Simon de Herrera and U.S. General James Wilkinson, the two military commanders of the regions, signed an agreement in November 1806, declaring the disputed area between the Arroyo Hondo (Calcasieu River) and the Sabine River to the west to be "Neutral Ground." This area was understood to extend from the Gulf of Mexico to the south to the general area of the thirty-second parallel in the north. And while the agreement was not strictly speaking a "treaty," for the most part both parties respected the pact.

The Neutral Ground agreement had stipulated that the disputed territory was to be off-limits to soldiers and settlers from either country, though the latter continued to move into the area from both New Spain and the United States. Bands of highwaymen and other outlaws became so ubiquitous that the governments had even sent out joint military expeditions on several occasions to drive out criminals in 1810 and 1812.

The Adams-Onis Treaty of 1821 recognized the U.S. claim to the territory as far west as the Sabine River, but the general area, including the sections of East Texas on the other side of the Sabine River, remained dangerously lawless. The construction of Fort Jesup in 1821 in western Louisiana was a response, though the small number of soldiers had a limited effect. As Two Hawks knew, solitary travelers and isolated families remained keenly vigilant if they wished to remain alive.

Chapter 5

"Two Hawks!" a man shouted, bounding over. "You old dog, where you been all this time?"

The young man looked familiar, but the old Caddo was cautious, shaping his expression into the confusion and loss of a stupid old red man.

"You—Two Hawks! It is I, Peter Hays, grown up and a man, *sixteen*. Surely you remember us?"

The old man's eyes tightened into focus, his mouth downturned into a faint grin. "You get all the honey out of that Tupelo, Mr. Peter, or you leave some for the bear?"

"Ha-ha, old one, I always leave some of whatever it is—I have forgotten nothing of what you told us."

"And the death of the Indian woman, She-de-a, you have kept that memory, too?"

Two Hawks thought back to his last encounter with the woman. In the spring, years ago, the Caddo squaw had caught him off guard, had struck him down with a stone from behind a storeroom door before he had even recognized who she was, hadn't even recognized her after swimming back into consciousness until she had begun to speak: "Oh, you were so wise, so good, permitting Bintah to maintain the nobility of his family, permitting him to mourn the loss of his beloved son, Nao'tsi, but you did not know his brave son as I did, as a woman did, married five rounds of seasons and no children, every woman and man looking at *me*. But I proved them wrong, did I not?"

"You proved," Two Hawks said slowly, "only your own wicked spirit, and that should not bring forth others of its kind—"

"Oh, you saw to that, too, old man: after they beat me with sticks, especially those women who knew the way their men looked at me, I was driven out of the village with nothing, not even a knife, to wander, the nights cold and without a fire."

"And the child you carried? What happened to it?

"Tanaha, my young love, followed me the next day — he was always a good tracker—and we found some brief comfort in each other's arms, his tattoos bright and clear, his eyes brimming with tears, as I gave him back his life."

"What do you mean?"

"Tanaha gave me his knife. I wandered, survived on bugs and berries, snakes and mice. I drove a coyote off his kill, a fawn two days dead. I stole from traps, tried to steal a beaver, but an old white man caught me, took my knife I tried to gut him with."

"Was he the one who cut the notch in your nose, She-de-a?"

"Do you know what an old white trapper smells like? Do you know what he feels like, on me, in me, Two Hawks? Do you know of anything that could be worse?"

"As long as you can speak and think, it is not the worst ..." He looked at her, and in three steps she was across the dirt floor, lashed him back and forth on the face with her beaded medicine bag and stomped on his ankle.

She stepped back and continued: "You know nothing of what I have had to do, you filthy old owl—I have been passed from man to man, the stink of rancid fat and fish ground into my spirit."

"And the child?"

"And the child—and the *child*? Under a cutback on the upper Calcasieu River, the rain pouring down, I was watching the river rise, though it was only a matter of time until it swept me out of my pathetic refuge, my fluid having broken that morning, and I screamed and pushed, burrowed my feet in the hackberry roots, pushed and panted until it lay before me in a pool of fluid and blood, and then afterbirth. I lay back, ignored her cries—yes, saw it was a girl."

"And?"

"The rain was coming down, the river was roaring and tumbling, the muddy water rolling broken branches and trees along, but through the noise I heard the grunt and snort, felt the heavy footfalls of the bear through the mud and dirt, knew he was smelling the blood."

"What did you do?"

"What could I do? I already knew I had business in this world, old man. I bit through the cord, chewed through it, grabbed that red-faced squealing thing by the legs in one hand, not any heavier than a jackrabbit, and threw her out to the bear—I wish you could go to sleep at night hearing the sounds that bear made pulling her apart—but all the time I put your face before my memory's eye, seeing always who put me there."

Two Hawks worked his wrists, twisting them, pulling, trying to stretch the rawhide laces enough to wriggle free, but they did not stretch, cutting instead through his skin, and he felt the slickness of blood running down between his fingers. Perhaps the liquid would lubricate his efforts, he thought, and redoubled his work. She stared at him steadily, pleased.

"Work all you wish, Caddo. I cut and cured and chewed those laces myself, feeling my spit soaking into the skin that would bind you. I have planned this moment for a long time and want to taste your suffering."

"The pains you cause mean very little to me, She-de-a. My time is quickly passing. You only further soil your spirit—that is all."

"Is it, Two Hawks? Your spirit is so confident, so clean and ready to carry you safely into the next world?"

The old Caddo looked at the woman, her body and face so creased and worn by all the uses of this world, so marred and disfigured by her own hatred, her own purposes almost eating through into the backs of her eyes, twisting her smile, and he was saddened by what he saw there.

"My spirit is not without stain," he said, "but I have tried—"

"Tried means nothing," she said. "Only what you have done means anything. And sometimes you destroy the innocent in your hunt for the truth...your friends, those you love ... Madame Dupre—"

"What do you know of her, witch?"

"Ho, wise man, her 'husband,' was killed, but Two Hawks, solver of puzzles, the Caddo, moves forward, reveals the killer, and justice is done."

"I do what I can."

"But Claude Sarcelle, the man they hanged, the man you revealed—"

"Yes?"

"Did nothing but care about Monsieur Dupre and trust an old piece of Indian trash."

"You are wrong, woman. I found—"

"You found what I wanted you to find, what I placed there. I slipped Claude's knife under Dupre's last rib, found his kidney before he could utter a sound, and I smelled the garlic stink of Madame's dinner on his last breath. You hanged the wrong one, and his spirit will cloud your heart like a bitter smoke."

"O, witch you have become, I will find—"

"Nothing—you will find I am not finished yet. The way you strain against those bonds, you wish to be released? Oh, look, here is your knife, that famous old trade knife of yours so many recognize—lean forward and I will let you go."

And Two Hawks did as she asked, leaned forward and extended his bloody hands up behind his back, tensing himself, half-expecting her to drive the heavy blade between his ribs under the shoulder blades, under the fading tattoos of the two raptors that had shielded him so many seasons, but the rawhide quickly parted and she sprang back, smiling.

"Unfold those old hams and stand up, man. If I wanted you dead, you'd be cold already." She laughed, waving him back with his knife. "No, I want you to live, and dream bad dreams of hanged men, haunted dreams. Solve this puzzle ..." She backed up, now raising her voice into a shout. "No! Do not kill me!"

She-de-a thrust Two Hawks' knife deep into her own stomach as hands outside worked at the bolt on the oak door, finally wrenching the door inward, two white men lunging forward into the room.

"He has killed me," she said, falling backward against the logs of the storeroom and sitting, still clutching the hilt of the knife protruding beneath her sagging breasts.

Looking over at Two Hawks standing in the small room, his bloody hands hanging at his sides, one of the men drew a heavy flintlock pistol from his sash: "Ho, old fellow, I see you now. I heard Madame Dupre listened to you about Sarcelle before the man was hanged. I trust you have a wondrous story to tell me this time, eh? Is that your knife sticking out of that squaw—it belong to you? That your knife?"

All three men turned to look at She-de-a, whose dark eyes burned into Two Hawks' face and slowly closed, her hands falling away from the bloody wooden hilt of the knife. The flow of blood out of the mouth-like gash, still holding the blade, ceased.

"That is my knife, he said, "but—"

"Cease—I do not need to hear your tale now, Indian. We will all listen to your story before the rope is tight. Come along to the Commander." The young Texian motioned for Two Hawks to precede him out the storehouse door.

The other man pointed to the woman's body: "What do we do with this?"

Walking toward the door out of which the old Indian had just stepped, the other turned back: "She will not turn too quickly in this weather—leave her be. And where ..." he suddenly said, seeing Two Hawks step to the side around the north corner of the storehouse.

"You—stop!" he shouted, jumped around the corner and aimed his pistol at the receding tattooed back.

The clack of his pistol's falling hammer told him the powder in the flash pan had become too damp to ignite. After glimpsing down in frustration and back up again, he was ready to give pursuit, but the still wall of greenery not three steps away gave no hint as to what direction the Caddo had taken.

"Well, dammee, Joseph!" he said to his companion now framed in the doorway. "How did he simply disappear like that? We'll go to the trading office and report—no, just leave her. They will know what to do with the body. I do not want to touch her. Did you see that old man *move*? Like a ghost."

But Two Hawks had merely stepped into the thick temperate forest undergrowth and dropped to the ground, pulling a heavy layer of dead leaves and branches over himself, lying perfectly still until the two young frontiersmen had gone.

He rose, shook off the detritus and swiftly slid back into the log room.

"Woman," he said patiently, "the spirits that take you now will bring you nothing but more pain." He pulled her medicine bag from around her bent neck and slowly drew out his knife from its wet sheath.

Moments later, he wound along a narrow game trail near town that led north of the settlement.

Chapter 6

"I have now—we always believed you. The others? Everyone soon forgot. The stabbing of another Indian, even of a woman, by another Indian—like the death of another deer or bear—of little consequence. You know how most of us think all the Indians are the same ..."

"You have grown to have those ideas, Mr. Peter?"

"Stop that *Mr.* Peter-poor-shuffling-old-red-man act. You sound like one of those old boys down by the post begging whiskey."

"Your sisters?" Two Hawks remembered the girls, remembered

them still as small children ...

"Oh, I do so wish the rain would cease," Rachel had said, seasons and seasons ago. Even at nine years old, she made serious pronouncements rather than simple statements. "Mother, it is so sad in this house without Father, and we have not been able to find suitable activities for our children outside," referring to her and her sister's dolls.

"Child," Margaret chided, "the rain makes everything grow—"

"Not me," Peter interrupted. "I cannot run or hunt or fish—the old rain should go away, and then Two Hawks could show me how to get the honey out of that tupelo tree he told me about."

The aging Caddo had come up out of his thoughts like an otter breaking the surface of a still pond. He creased his eyes in a smile, and said, "There was a round of seasons—"

"Why do you never say 'a year' like we do?" Pamela said, looking up from the tiny wool dress she was making for her doll.

"One year is one," Two Hawks said. "I see nothing *one* about a round of seasons."

"But you said 'a round,' that's just one—" said Peter.

"True," the Indian said, "and there is one Calcaseau River, but it is never the same so there is always more than one—"

"Fine, a 'round of seasons,'" Peter said, knowing that a story was coming. His sisters came over to sit on the boards of the porch closer to where the old man always sat on a dry patch of earth under the roof's overhang, the drumming of the rain dripping from the roof, a soft wall of sound enclosing them.

"A round of seasons," he began. "Many seasons ago and far away toward where the sun goes down every day, at the end of what long ago were Caddo lands—" He noticed the children had begun to fidget, and raised his voice: "Everything was DYING!"

The three children looked up, their breaths caught, and opened their mouths. Children were the same everywhere, the man thought, smiling to himself, and continued: "The corn had dried up in the gardens before the ears had fully formed, the squashes' leaves sounded in the wind like rattles made by bad spirits, and the very small children cried because their mothers' breasts were drying up—"

"Eeew—that is just not nice." Pamela made a face.

"But in some way, the people had made the spirits angry," Two

25

Hawks said. "The spirits would not sweep the heavy clouds with their wings, and bring the rain. For many, many days it had not rained—even the animals left the land when the creeks and ponds dried up, and the medicine makers had sung their prayers and smoked their offerings to the four directions. The village elders had never seen the land so cracked and dry, the children so thin and weak ..."

"And—and ...?" the girls said together.

But Two Hawks waited two breaths before beginning again: "One little girl, about your age, Pamela, but with long thick black hair, once very shiny but now almost grey in its dryness, had a doll, a *kachina* they called them then, that she had spent many days making with a care and attention the others thought beyond her years. Every time she combed her hair, she carefully collected whatever strands were caught in the teeth of the horn comb; she put aside soft bits of fur that were discarded from robes or bedding, scraps of well-tanned clothing her mother could find no use for, a few brightly colored trade beads her father presented to her as a special gift, and in early spring, after a startled buck's sharp hooves had severed a fibrous thick stalk of corn, she pulled the leaves and stripped the central stem of its supple strings."

He stopped, and gave Peter and Rachel and Pamela time to let their imaginations construct the doll.

"Her kachina was wondrous to behold. The doll was soft but shapely, fringed, and sewn with cherished horsehair, the head covered with the little girl's lustrous black hair that fell in a tight braid behind, bright green glass beads for her eyes."

"The doll's eyes were blue beads," Rachel said. "I can see them ..."

"Perhaps blue," the Caddo conceded. "And she held the doll and loved it and carried it everyplace. But one night her father sent her to the dwelling of the shaman, the priest, with a small quarter of the starved deer he had traveled more than one day to find, the medicine man clucking in gratitude as he carefully fed the fire he kept burning day and night to remain in touch with the spirits."

"She gave him the doll?" Peter thought he knew where this story was going.

Two Hawks looked at the three children, also noticing the mother's still face in the doorway, her face framed with soft curls escaped from her chignon while cleaning the cabin.

"She returned to the dwelling of her family, leaned back against the bundles of reeds forming the walls, and tried to sleep. One by one, her brothers and sisters, finally her mother, and at last her father fell into a restless sleep. Still, she stared into the embers of the fire, looked at her cherished companion, the green bead eyes catching the faint light, and saw they were the color of deep water. Her tears ran down her face because she knew what was to come."

"She gave the medicine man the doll!" Pamela said.

"All night she held her kachina," he said slowly. "And as the light first outlined the eastern trees, she went to the shaman's dwelling, quietly entered and knelt at the fire that always burned. The medicine man was awake but gave no sign. She smoothed down the hair on her doll's head one last time and lay her kachina's corn and leather body across the glowing embers and sobbed quietly as the fire awoke. Then she started and felt the elder's hand rest on her own head."

"'They will thank you, child,' he had said, and watched the dark clouds crowd the horizon later that day. And then it rained."

"That is a terrible, horrible sad story, Two Hawks," Rachel said.

The children stared out at the falling curtains of rain, and Margaret stepped forward, a question in her light eyes.

The children loved his stories, always listened in amazement, though the stories were so often sad.

"Why did you tell them that story?"

"We must not want the rain to stop," the elder man had said. "The cost may be great to start the rain again. Someone always pays for the rain"

Chapter 7

"Gone—Rachel married and gone to Opelousas, Pamela taken on as a nanny for friends of mother's in New Orleans, a huge city on the Mississippi River I went to visit—Two Hawks, you should see all the ships and keelboats." The excitement in the young man's voice charged the air, though Two Hawks understood little of what Peter spoke.

"And Madame—"

"Yes, *Madame Dupre*. I am Peter *Hays*, but Mother finds that calling herself Madame Dupre carries more weight. I do not resent that—as a woman with two dead husbands, so to speak, she does not have an easy time in the world of men—but Mother gets along. In fact, she is putting together a grand adventure for us ..."

The Caddo appeared to listen, though the sights and sounds, even the smells of the burgeoning settlement crowded in upon his vision, the passing mule-drawn wagon loaded with bales of cloud-white cotton, the young son of a planter trailed by an old negro shouldering a loaded pack, three girls in frilled dresses giggling and squealing at the mercantile window as if there were no more bears or snakes or treacherous men in the entire land under the eyes of stars. Even the smells of fresh sawn lumber and cooking rice seemed to assail his senses as hostile tribes from a swelling threat ...

"... and DeWitt's man has told Mother there are broad open prairies to the south, already stocked with wild Mesican cattle waiting to be claimed ..."

Two Hawks had seen these "cattle" to the south—with old moss-grown horns a tall man's outstretched arms wide, mean enough to drive a horn through a charging horse or even a bear. A wild animal was something to be reckoned with, a clean spirit to understand and embrace, whether it be a skunk or crow or even the mysterious spirit of the vanishing wolf. And the other animals, the cows or goats or horses, the chickens or pigs or dogs, the ones kept by the settlements, one could look into their eyes, read their spirits and *know* them for what they are, find a point of stability.

But the ones that live in the twilight realm, the animals that once began, lived, worked in the midst of the whites, the settlements, and had gone back to the wild places, those confused spirits were difficult to accommodate, in large part because their identity was confused. And Two Hawks understood with no small irony that he increasingly if not irrevocably fell into that group.

The cattle, "longhorns" they were called by the Texicans, seemed to have a burning eye of resentment, not in the same way that a deer or buffalo or even wildcat had, the truly wild animals fighting with the wild abandon of otherness. The cows, like a growing number of wild hogs encountered in the scrub forest rooting about for sustenance, seemed to glare at the humans with some deep feeling of blame, as if *knowing* what people really had done, wanted to do and take away from the animals' spirits—there appeared to be a clear hatred in their eyes that somehow the truly wild were too naïve to understand.

"… and the Colony's organizers would grant Mother one league of rich but undeveloped grazing land—think of it, Two Hawks, that is almost *seven square miles*, 4428 acres. I know, you understand little of such measurements, but that is more land than you can walk across in most of a morning. We would be rancheros, planters. I would be a gentleman!"

Looking down at his bunched and knotted forearm, the deep coffee tone of swamp water, the lightning tattoos only dim smears, Two Hawks could still make out the shape of a blue heron, head cocked like a pistol hammer, that he had picked out with a fishbone one afternoon, thought about the large blue herons wading in the shallows of the great sea to the south, their long thin legs sliding down still and soundless into the tepid marsh water, the long legs like sticks broken backward, hinges on smooth bark. Why are they not hinged forward, like his own legs? If his legs bent backward instead of forward at the knee, would he not be a ghost-like stalker, his feet sliding forward, low and foremost, into the leaves like knives sheathed and then unsheathed back out, sheathed and unsheathed silently in the forest—but the image entire arose in his mind of himself an old Indian scissoring forward through the undergrowth on giant blue heron legs, and he stifled a laugh and thought back to his first tattoo…

Even now, so many seasons past, often in times of tension, he felt a stirring over the skin of his upper back where the great bone blades protected his vital parts from behind. At times the sensation was almost a shudder, a delicate sweeping over the skin, the flutters of two pairs of wings, but at times his very muscles felt torn, rent by great hooked talons as the hawks commanded his attention and concern.

And at such times, his memories boiled to the surface like a large bass flashing its silver sides over a swimming frog, a quick glimpse but clear and entire. He remembered lying face down along the fallen cypress trunk near their village, the bark smoothed away, his young arms and legs draped over into the soft spring grass … and the pain.

His father, Oat, had reminded him of the pain he had seen on the faces of the other boys close to being men, had reminded him to always meet pain with endurance, the endurance that permits no feeling, with an apathy toward misfortune that becomes a man.

Other than the tiny experimental marks the boys had inflicted on each other and themselves in imitation of their elders, this had been Two Hawks' first and remained his most powerful tattoo. His father and the medicine man worked quietly, seriously, over the boy's back for half of the morning, tapping the needles with short sticks, using hollow and sharpened heron bones and the thicker but very sharp canine teeth of a young opossum to open the design. They wiped the welling blood away almost until it ceased, then rubbing under the skin the black ash mixed with bear fat.

The tears had welled from his eyes, regardless of how hard he tried to prevent them, but his gaze and the set of his mouth remained impassive, his mind reaching like a hand into his future as a man.

He recalled the weeks following that day as the burning pain gradually subsided to a sometimes maddening itch as his back crusted over and the skin healed beneath puckering scales that he rubbed off on clean grass or soaked in the creek still chilled by the cold nights of early spring.

But that initial tattoo had finally grown over with new skin, Two Hawks still feeling as though only a handful of days had passed, the slide of Kah'aih's fingers over his bare back one night as the family sat around the glowing embers of their fire, their shadows in bizarre shapes cast out onto the inner walls of their Caddo house. He could smell the bear meat and venison drying in long strips up near where the fire's smoke made its way out past the bundles of reeds and straw coming together. The beehive-shaped dwelling had been made in the ancient Caddo way, built by his father a number of seasons before Two Hawks had been born, still strong and clean and warm.

Kah'aih, his in'a, the same word used alike for mother and his mother's sister, as she was, had slid her hands over his back as he gazed, seemingly unaware, into the embers, one piece of oak stump breaking open, the scarlet coal within staring back like an eye.

"The color is coming to the surface like black blood," she had said. "They will shield you, these wings of night."

And he had hastened the following day to see what she had seen, leaving the village near mid-day, ostensibly to check his snares down near the river, but locating the small catch-pond he had remembered to the north. Pine and hickory gradually thinned, replaced by several old cypress trees, their blunt, rounded roots emerging like the fingers of the dead, spirits waiting to draw him under.

30

The surface of the disk of water was unmoving and lay like a giant imitation of those small mirrors he had seen in Nacogdoches on trading visits, the bright sunlight dappled and reflected between the trees' feathery branches. The boy crept out along one low-draped branch that stretched over the water, hung himself downward by hands and legs as close to the water as he could, and craned his neck around, his breath catching as his back was reflected up to his hungry eyes.

The dark forms tattooed on his skin seemed to emerge from the surface of the water, to visibly move over his shoulder blades like raptors mantling their prey, shielding it from prying eyes.

Chapter 8

"... in three weeks! You old Caddo—you haven't heard anything of what I have said. Come talk to Mother—" said Peter.

"The Karankawa," said Two Hawks. "What do you know of the Karankawa?"

"Oh, I have heard of those, southwest of your folks, peaceful, they say—"

"No, not Tonkawas. The Karankawas, along the big water—"

"Gulf of Mexico?"

"You call it that ... Would Madame Dupre remember this old Indian?"

"Two Hawks, you don't understand. Even after these years, sometimes I find her staring off over the trees to the west and saying something such as 'I wonder where he is, Peter. Does he still live?' And I know who she speaks about. But come to the house, this evening at six o'clock—sorry, at the time the sun falls below the trees. See? I still recall how you see things."

"I will come, sir." Two Hawks tried to sound formal and respectful, as he assumed Peter Hays to be now head of the house.

"Mother will be very excited ... Well, old one, I must speak to a man about a horse." Peter turned on his heel and marched purposefully down the packed dirt street, thinking later he had omitted telling the Caddo that they lived in a larger house now, the house of Felix Trudeau, recently deceased. But remembering the capacity of Two Hawks' mind, both from memory and from what his mother had recounted, Peter would bet a beaver hat the old man would find his way. The young man also decided he would not tell his mother about the anticipated visitor. Wouldn't she be surprised?

Later that afternoon, Margaret Hays Dupre lifted the cornbread out of her cherished cast iron pan and set it on the oak board to rest, turning back to the fireplace on the stone flags to lift the lid from a pot of fresh lima beans stewing with two pork shanks she had received from helping her neighbor butcher a hog struck by a freight wagon. The bouquet of herbed stew and toasted cornbread filled the small kitchen room, which was detached by a breezeway from the main house to reduce the risk of a fire spreading to the rest of the dwelling. She stepped over the timber threshold beyond the heavy plank door, moving toward the main house to call her son to supper, glanced to her left and froze, audibly catching her breath.

Two Hawks stood at the mortised corner of the log wall, expressionless, in anticipation of her reaction. He knew that every season of the intervening years had been carved on his form—he was indeed feeling older but still felt an almost boyish anxiety that he might not be welcome.

"Oh, Two Hawks," she said.

A bit older, he noted, but still a young woman, her sky-colored eyes tightened in alarm but then softened, and her mouth turned up in a smile.

"You have come." She sounded almost as if she had asked for, even expected, his return.

"My rifle needed work, so I brought it to Mr. Corey. I saw Peter—he asked me to come." But the reason rang as hollow as it was.

"Oh, that mischievous boy. He told me nothing."

Two Hawks was embarrassed. "I did not mean—"

"Please. I am glad to see you, old one. You must come in and share supper with us and tell us everything ... Where is that scoundrel son of mine?"

"Mother," Peter said as he rounded the corner of the main house from the small storage barn in back, "I told him about DeWitt's Colony. Perhaps he would come with us?"

"Invite Two Hawks inside," she motioned to the door, then wiped her hands on her flour sack apron. "Set another place and help me carry the supper—yes, thank you, sir," she said as the Caddo offered a piece of brick tea from his pouch. "Tea sounds like a wonderful idea."

During the meal, Two Hawks perched nervously on the delicate French chair, expecting it any moment to collapse under his weight into a pile of sticks, relishing the beans and cornbread, highly seasoned fare compared to his usual roasted small game lightly salted from his meager supply, though he did enjoy adding wild onions and spiced peppers when he could. He had even tried roasting a wild turkey stuffed with black-berries and last year's pecans once, with some success.

Later, Margaret and Peter in rush-seated chairs on the porch, their guest choosing to sit on the edge of the plank floor, half-concealed from the street, the two men shared a corn-cob pipe—the woman having a slightly smaller clay version. Rich sweet smoke from fresh-cured tobacco drifted up in waved layers like oily seas in the still evening.

"So, my old friend," she began, "what do you think of the plan? I must make a way for myself and my son here in this world, and in Natchitoches the opportunities are, well, small ... I have heard so many things about how rich the land is, how even a widow may build something, and of course there are Indians. Tell us what you know of the red tribes south and west of here. Dr. Sibley, who as you know was appointed by the U.S. as the designated Indian Agent for this area for a number of years, he knew about Indians as far south as Matagorda Bay, but Sibley is, well, cautious in his opinions."

"The doctor is a great friend to the Indian," Two Hawks began, "and he has made peace with many groups. The Tonkawa—"

"I told him, Mother, but he says the Karankawas—"

"Hush, boy," she said. "Don't interrupt." Looking over at Two Hawks with a faint smile, she added, "The young are so rushed. Please, take the time you need."

"The Tonkawas," the Caddo began again, "are a good people. The more in the direction of where the big water meets the land south of here, and the sun goes to sleep each day, the danger grows."

"Let me add, my friend," Margaret put in, "that the government down there will not permit settlement or deeded land any closer than ten leagues of the coast. That is as far as from Natchitoches to the Sabine."

"That is good. As Peter says, I know something of the Indians along the water there—they are old enemies of the Caddo, of anyone. Only three rounds of seasons ago ..." His jaw tightened at the memory, and his hand strayed to his lower back.

"Tell us, Two Hawks," Peter said, recalling the old man's stories. "Tell us exactly what happened."

Chapter 9

"My journey had begun as a spirit trail, remembering one my father shared long ago, the end fingers of a ground mist reaching south, and one morning, the surface of my cooling tea had delicately trembled on the fallen log, the mat of damp oak leaves transmitting motion, and I had tensed himself."

Half a handful of blue jays had stilled their screeching a short time ago, telling the elder Caddo that something had drawn stealthily near from behind—he gave no sign of noticing until the keen edge of a blade pressed into his neck.

From the hand pressed down onto his shoulder, the flat putrid musk of brackish mud and alligator fat told Two Hawks to whisper in the halting Spanish that in those days often served as common language between bands, "I am no enemy to Karankawas—"

"Your body pictures say Caddo," had come the sighing lilt of the voice behind him. "We kill Caddo here."

Knowing many of the stories told up north of the ways in which the Karankawa relished consuming the spirits of their captives while the prisoners were still alive, at least for a time, the older man thought but only briefly about twisting away and overcoming the youth behind him. But he was no longer the Two Hawks who had more than once turned Osage or Kiowa over his shoulder and in one smooth motion had searched for the living heart beneath the ribs with a sharp knife, holding the blade firm as the beats slowed and ebbed away with the lights in their eyes.

The moments from the past flitted by like frighted minnows on a quiet creek, and he spoke in measured tones, "I am yours, but bring me to where you may share and celebrate my leaving with your brothers—"

"Lean back those withered limbs, old man, and I'll strap you up for camp," the other man said. "But I fear I will be chewing a chattering old crow instead of a man."

34

And so it wore on through the middle of the day, Fish Eye (as Two Hawks learned his captor's name) and the older Caddo winding through the thick brush on game trails, the old man sometimes stumbling over roots or marl outcroppings, his bound arms doing nothing to keep his balance or break his falls.

But as the sun slid slowly down the sky, when Two Hawks should have felt the ire and hatred of his enemy's gaze burning into his back, when the old man readied himself for the mocking kicks and pushes on tight bends in the trails, he felt nothing, a spirit elsewhere. The Caddo's puzzled questions were met only by sullen silence.

Late in the day, the two men reached the band of Karankawas on a small watercourse that the Spanish called the Tres Palacios River, near where it runs into the upper reaches of Matagorda Bay. A stand of pecan and stunted live oaks helped shelter the sandy clearing splotched with wickiups, saplings bent over and pushed into the soft soil. Woven mats and scattered animal skins shielding the inhabitants from the brightness of the low southern sun and the lashing of bay-born squalls.

Along with the typical smells of decaying animal refuse and old fires, Two Hawks' nostrils flared briefly with the scent of scorched tar, with memories that these southern bands use bitumen collected on the beach to seal their clay pots, very crude cooking containers compared to the elaborate fired and painted wares of the Caddo.

And then, as the pair strode deeper into the clearing and neared a large mound of fly-swarmed oyster shells, the smell of hastily emptied bowels and bellies rolled thick through the still camp like the passing of a hand draped with dead hair. And the pounding *absence* of sound, loud and pulsing as a drum, made itself felt, the absence of the daily rounds of family life—no children calling, laughing, or mothers murmuring, scolding, not even an alerted dog or clatter of a spoon dropped from an elder's hand—the silence and languid, lethargic movements of the inhabitants pressed in upon Two Hawks more sharply than had the blade of Fish Eye's knife.

Here was sickness, of a kind the Caddo had not encountered for half a man's days ... he remembering one hot summer's trip with a handful of other Caddo young men, carrying deer hides to Fort St. Jean Baptiste, near Natchitoches, to trade for those flat bricks of European tea they had grown so fond of ...

A stinging prod from Fish Eye's knife, drawing blood, brought Two Hawks' attention quickly back to his present predicament, and he sat where he was told, in front of one of the larger brush-covered huts, near a deeply creased and sun-blackened old man whose ear hoops draped almost to his bowed shoulders, a peccary tusk piercing the flesh beneath his lower lip. Other than a large trade knife in a beaded sheath held to his waist by a thong, the man wore nothing.

Fish Eye began: "I have captured this tricky Caddo a day's walk to the north, where he was making a potion in a trader's cup, spying on Karankawa land. He is old and stringy—still, we will gain strength from consuming his spirit."

"Ah," was the old man's measured response, before swinging his bowed head to the captive and looking up.

The old man's expression and eyes reminded Two Hawks of an old wolf he had encountered once far to the north, the wolf's hind half caught under a deadfall set for larger game. As the Caddo had drawn closer, the wolf, at least a day or two in the trap, had growled briefly and then stared into Two Hawks' eyes in pain, in confusion, but in a resignation of his dark journey ahead. The animal, almost pleading for the Caddo to bring this path to a close, took the lance and dropped his head, the man watching the spirit move on.

But Two Hawks also knew that many tribes saw the intricate governance and traditions of the Caddo Confederacy as a system of trickery and deceit, so he sat still and waited.

At last, the old man spoke: "What are you called, Caddo?"

"I am Two Hawks, and mean no harm to the Karankawa."

"A hand of seasons ago I heard of a Caddo with a name such as you say," the old man said, "a truth-eater, they called him, a strange older man who found truth and ate it, the hard, bitter truth, and then went away..." The old man's gaze drifted off over the bay, the setting sun squeezing his eyes almost shut.

"I have been called such—" Two Hawks began, memories clouding his vision, but was cut off by the younger one.

"The Caddo is lying—he will say anything. We must kill him for our strength," he pleaded. His first captive, he feared, was becoming too comfortable with Blue Heron, his father.

But the elder Karankawa simply said, "Ah," and turned back to the

Caddo. "The truth is all around us here, Caddo man, and it has already taken most of our children—too much truth for one man to consume, even were you the Two Hawks I had once heard of ..."

"Sometimes there are more truths than one," Two Hawks said. "Sometimes one truth bears another, or even more—"

"You hear, father, you hear how he will twist and lie to stay alive—he is mine, I tell you," and Fish Eye caught his breath. He knew his passion had carried him too far.

"Ah," Heron raised his head, "he *tells* me. What do you tell me, Caddo? I cannot stop my children dying— will your eaten spirit keep them alive?"

A male cardinal ping-ping-pinged twice atop a pecan sapling nearby before Two Hawks spoke: "I can tell you nothing, old one, you know that. I can say that I am on a journey that I do not see an end to here. I can say that I may remember another sickness similar to this one, but I need to see your life here to know. I may be able to learn—"

"Stop him, father. He wants only to deceive us and slip away."

"Ah, son, wouldn't you? But if he can know what ails us—"

"Permit me three days," Two Hawks said, "starting tomorrow. Tie me to your son Fish Eye if you will, and let me ... *see*. Then do with me what you will."

"You have three days, Caddo Two Hawks, and my son will—*quiet, Fish Eye*—my son will do as you need."

The moist morning breeze coming off the salt marshes nearby roused Two Hawks awake. And he began to stretch his stiff arms, but was quickly reminded of the wet thongs that held his palms together. The earth, even the sand here, is getting harder, he thought, but not too hard. Knowing the solution to that problem held a mystery like an open bowl.

He sat up and crab-walked outside toward the fire, rubbing the crust from his eyes, seeing the family groups of Karankawa begin to busy themselves around him in preparing for the day, but with a dreadful lack of energy or cheer, a distinct loathing for the coming day.

As Two Hawks quietly made water in the brush beyond the clearing, under the watchful gaze of Fish Eye, a keening wail arose from one of the near wikiups as a woman emerged, the grease on her cheeks already streaked with tears, a limp child draped over her outstretched arms. She fell to her knees in the sand, her hair brushing the still boy.

The Caddo moved toward the kneeling form, restrained by Fish Eye until he reassured the younger with a glance.

"Please, young woman, please," Two Hawks said, and Blue Heron told her that the stranger meant no harm.

The Caddo squatted next to the mother and child, gently extended his bound hands, and softly pinched the skin on the young boy's upper arm. The flesh peaked and remained upraised. When the boy's forearm was faintly scratched by the Caddo's fingernail, a dry trail of white skin followed. Together with the wrinkles around the young boy's eyes, his skin response began to tell a story, though the bowels' contents would add more clay to the bowl that would hold the solution.

Two Hawks' eyes were caught by an older woman reentering the camp, looking very weak and frail, and the Caddo, Fish Eye in tow, back-trailed the woman by following the disturbed dew through the low brush and broom straw. The woman's diminishing pool of diarrhea was soaking into the detritus near several others, and the watery milk-like color and consistency further confirmed his growing belief. One more piece and he would be ready to smooth his vessel into a shape that might contain an anodyne.

Some time later, back in the main clearing of the camp, having eaten several strips of blackened fish, washed down with yaupon tea, the Caddo met the gaze of Heron, who shuffled over with a large brown bowl, sealed on the outside and bottom with sea tar. "Water, Caddo man? You must keep your strength for us." His eyes creased in humor.

Chapter 10

"Ah," Two Hawks remembered he had said, and grinned, having used the same intonation as was the other's habit, and then stopped, his hands coming up to take the bowl. Handfuls of seasons were swept from his eyes, and he was again inside the rough log gates of the French fort near Natchitoches all those years ago with Yellow Arm and Three Bears and the others, burdened with their rolls of hides, moving toward the trading room where a number of other men, some of other tribes, squatted on the ground in groups of three or four, waiting their turns to make their purchases or exchanges.

The young Caddo had noticed the fresh mounds of graves outside the fort and the indistinct scent of sickness but were too eager for their tea and visions of new trade goods, their attention also dulled by the thick odors of the freshly tanned deer hides they carried.

But then, after dropping his stack of rolled furs on the ground, the young Two Hawks began to see the numbers of white people more wandering than walking about their business, many with the pallor of recovering illness. Most of the graves he had noticed were small, and he now began to see the absence of children. Also returning to him was the sight of several French men carting in barrels of water, a curious sight since he knew the foreigners had a hole in the ground inside the fort for water.

Even then more curious than his companions, Two Hawks had convinced them after their trades, a sizable stack of the deep umber European tea bricks stamped with strange markings, along with four steel needles and a wood-handled trade knife safely stowed in their pouches, to camp a short distance from the fort. As his friends fished in one of the bayous that wound to the Rive Rouge, the young Caddo had returned on two successive days to the fort to study recent occurrences.

He noted one man called Docteur Marchand by the French, who made regular visitations to the barracks and officers' quarters, as well as to several nearby cabins. At last, the young Caddo's curiosity winning over his inhibitions, he had stepped forward as the man left a cottage not far from the fort's gates and asked in a combination of French and Spanish what the Frenchman was doing.

"Le Cholera," the doctor had said, surprised by the Indian's questions and by the glint of fascination in his dark eyes. "We have had cholera but are recovering."

"This illness," Two Hawks said. "It is a bad spirit you eat with meat or squash?"

"Water," Marchand had said. "Bad water," and motioned for the Caddo to follow him.

Dr. Marchand had taken Two Hawks on his afternoon circuit, showing him the surviving youngsters and one recent infection, the latter given over to violent spasms of vomiting and diarrhea, the stool a milky liquid. The boy had already begun to lose weight and luster, his skin dry and wrinkling to the touch, a result of a rapid loss of fluid, the doctor explained. He would soon die, the doctor said, unless he could ingest and retain more water and minerals.

"But why is water bad? We must have water," the Caddo said.

"Good water—we must have good water," Marchand repeated, explaining that the water from the fort's well had been dug too close to the latrine wells. Once a new water source had been found and the ill prompted to consume foods to replace important minerals the bodies needed, the outbreak had begun to wane.

And for some reason the doctor himself could not have explained, as he had shaken the serious young Caddo's hand in departure, he pressed a flat disk of glass into the man's hand. Two Hawks later found that when he looked through the glass, objects were larger.

All of these memories passed before Two Hawks' eyes in the span of two long breaths, his vision cleared, and he dropped his hands to his lap. "No water for me, Heron. But show me where the water comes from."

The three men—the Caddo and the younger and elder Karankawa—walked in the direction of the setting sun along a worn path and down through reeds to the bank of the river, within sight of its emptying into the shallow flats of Matagorda Bay. Stones were piled into a series of steps so they could draw water from the swifter movement away from the muddy bank. The river moved languidly, not more than a stone's throw wide.

Toward the opposite bank, caught on the dead limbs of a flood-born cottonwood, a fresh oak branch hung momentarily before tumbling on downstream, its sharp cut end clearly visible.

"Blue Heron, who shares your land?"

"Some outcast Spanish men, turned away from the presidio, have come to trap and look for tallow cattle, but they are lazy and will soon give up and be gone from Karankawa land."

"Take me close so I may watch them."

Fish Eye objected, feeling his captive may yet escape by calling out to the Spaniards, but Two Hawks said, "I will not betray your trust," and Blue Heron placed his hand upon his son's shoulder.

Later, Two Hawks drew closer to the Spaniards' encampment, close to the riverbank, wet with mud. These men, less than two hands' full, were unkempt, their camp disorganized, haphazard. Their long hair and beards were matted, the men talking loudly, arguing, so they heard nothing of the others' approach. The Caddo had experienced Spanish law many times, often cruel, sometimes soft, often confusing and mysterious, but Spanish law imposed an iron will in its people that sent them on arduous journeys, carved out habitations from the living rock, created wondrous utensils and weapons, all of which were frequently detrimental to Two Hawks' own people. But these Spanish men here followed no Spanish law, he could see, followed no law of any kind, not even one of their own agreement. These men were like stray dogs, rabid dogs, burdened by domestication, too lost to find a master, an infection.

Two Hawks waited, still as the tree he leaned against, for the first half of the afternoon. Four times he saw men clutch their bellies and waddle down to the riverbank, squat, and empty their loose bowels into the water. He had seen enough.

Back in front of the Karankawa huts, the Caddo sat and mused about his predicament. He knew what he must do, but he also knew that *his* time might pass before they believed him.

Blue Heron sat an arm's length away, silent, trying to share the vision this stranger saw off across the bay, as three pelicans drifted low over the still water, wing tips touching the surface.

"I can help you, perhaps not help you all," Two Hawks began, his voice sounding like it came from far away. "You do not yet believe me ... Permit me to show you. I will choose one of your sick children, and you and I and Fish Eye will carry the child away to a new camp. There I will show you what you must do."

"Father, I do not trust this Caddo who talks tricks—"

"Ah," Heron began, saddened at the future without children. "This Caddo here is the smallest we can lose."

The next morning they set out, those three, with a young girl, Sandpiper, who had been sick for two days, her body quickly wasting away, shriveling up, from the almost constant evacuation from mouth and bowels. They took turns carrying her in a sling, the other two laden with blue crabs, pecans, three sweet potatoes, and a pair of turkey hens they had snared in the dawn hour.

After Two Hawks had questioned him at length the night before, Blue Heron led them two hours' walk around the bay to the south, inland to where a stream wound through a sandy grove of oaks, their massive limbs draping to the ground. The men built a fire pit and followed the Caddo's instructions.

The crabs and turkey were roasted, the potatoes soon cracking open in the coals nearby, and bowls of water were carried from the stream. These well-cooked ingredients were mixed with the crushed pecan meats and fed to the girl, along with copious amounts of water. She kept them down only for a short time. More water was given.

And so the evening wore on, the fire replenished, the trips to the stream frequent, the practice repeated throughout the night and halfway through the morning of the next day.

Soon after dawn, her eyes closed and her shallow chest ceased its feverish rhythm—Two Hawks thought, she's gone—and the two Karankawa looked at him as one looks at a passing spirit. Then she started, caught a breath, and a tear slid down her cheek.

"Oh, I will thank dreaming," Two Hawks said.

As the morning wore on, Sandpiper held down a little more water each time and a gradual change could be perceived in the skin on her thigh, a softening, and it slowly began to spring back to the gentle pinch of the Caddo.

"The water," Blue Heron said, at last. "The water in the river is poisoned from the Spaniards' filth."

"Any man's filth. Learn and do not drink where any animal passes food. But see, too, Heron—you must make your children keep the water or they will dry up and die."

"I believe you, Caddo Two Hawks," the old man said. He said something to his son then in their language, and the Karankawa stepped off several paces to begin what grew into a lengthy and heated exchange between father and son. Two Hawks knew his life was being weighed and thought back over a long and often painful journey. Perhaps his path ended here, under the arms of this old tree, the moss on the limbs inviting, beckoning.

The Karankawa came forward, Blue Heron facing him. Quickly Fish Eye seized the Caddo's upper arms in a powerful grip from behind, as the father drew his knife, a flat stone in his other hand. Heron looked into Two Hawks' eyes, his own creasing into a smile, before he struck the Caddo on the side of the head with the stone, stunning him to his knees, reaching down, pinching a soft roll of flesh at the waist and, in two lightning swipes, freed a piece of flesh a finger thick and as long.

Two Hawks shook his head then to bring consciousness back, felt Fish Eye's grip release his arms, and struggled to his feet. Heron held his gaze as he handed that small piece of Two Hawks to his son.

"Go, Caddo Two Hawks. We will find good water for the remainder. I could not leave my son with nothing from his first captive. But I told him, in truth, consume too much of your spirit, and I would lose a son to the pain I see behind your eyes."

Later that day, the wound had crusted over as Two Hawks paced south, and he knew Blue Heron had cut what was not needed for his path.

Chapter 11

Madame Dupre had told him that in fact Dr. Sibley was very much still breathing, that the doctor had been in politics and had gone to Texas and recently returned to live in his old house on the hill near the big bend in the bayou.

Always approaching a situation obliquely whenever possible, having in that method frequently a route to either retreat or change direction, Two Hawks sat under a large water oak behind the doctor's house for only a short time before a house servant, coming to hang the morning wash out to dry and sun, approached with suspicion.

Rachael, an Ebo slave, having grown up in New Orleans until Dr. Sibley brought her to Natchitoches as a late teen, had had little experience with Indians, but she had heard stories. Some said that the Indians were always looking to carry off women, white or black, to serve the natives in their horrible rituals until the women perished. Others said the Indians loved the black people and offered freedom from the hardships of slavery, welcoming runaways into the tribes. She did not know what to think, but she knew that the doctor and his aging wife had treated her reasonably well, not really like a slave at all but like a servant who lived there, even giving her a few coins now and again to buy ribbons or candy. Miz Eudalie had also begun to teach her to read the Bible, even though she knew it was forbidden for most slaves to read.

This old man squatting in the yard had some fearsome tattoos, his skin shining with unwashed skin oil, or something worse. Yet, when he slowly turned his head in her direction and raised his eyes, she felt no trepidation, nor any sorrow either, as he looked at her in some way, she thought, as another person, as understood and accepted. Still, she had learned at a very young age that there were an infinite number of tricky men.

"What you doing here?" she said, in a challenging tone.

The man creased his eyes in amusement. "Tell Dr. Sibley an old Caddo man has come—"

"I do not *tell* Dr. Sibley nothing, old man."

"Say old Two Hawks is dying behind his house," he said, and dropped his chin onto his chest.

Alarmed, Rachael set the basket of wash down in the leaves and acorns under the tree, gathered her skirt, and rushed back to the house.

Scarce minutes later, the aging doctor emerged through the back door, clambored down the steps, and strode quickly to the seated Caddo, who raised his eyes and grinned. "Ah, Dr. Sibley—you do not want dead Indians behind your house?"

"Two Hawks, you old Caddo dog!" The doctor laughed and put his hands on his hips. "I should have known. You'll not die behind some white man's house but alone on a hill somewhere, like a ragged old wolf ..."

"We are all always dying, doctor, maybe we two closer to the ground than many," he responded, but still his heart was gladdened to hear this man salt his talk with old Caddo expressions.

"But come in, man," Sibley said, and then noted how Two Hawks drew back away from the door. "I know, you old hound, you do not like to enter white men's dwellings, feels like you're an old fox climbing into a trap, but come—I have things to show you in my study, and I want to hear about your adventures, I might even say 'cases,' in the cool of the house."

And so the two men sat in the doctor's study and wiled away most of the day, their low voices occasionally interrupted briefly when, at the direction of the doctor's wife, Rachael brought in smoked passenger pigeon and a refilled pitcher of cold well water.

Initially excited, Sibley showed his old friend the brass tubes of a microscope—Two Hawks gratified but not genuinely surprised at the wriggling life a few drops of stagnant water held. They both had long understood the plenitude that the seemingly invisible spaces of this world contained, though there was pleasure in seeing the myriad shapes and designs.

This discussion naturally led to their reminiscing about the dysentery outbreak those many years ago, the glass pitcher of water sweating with condensation on the table between them, and Two Hawks thinking that the opportunity had arisen for seeking the doctor's opinion and advice about that territory west of the Neutral Ground that was increasingly being called "Texas" by those people whose aspirations looked west.

Sibley related experiences of his own excursion with James Long into Spanish Texas not too many years earlier, saying that perhaps if he were a younger man, the opportunities seemed to be ripe, though he mentioned that he himself had soon returned to the relative comfort and ease of Natchitoches, noting as well that he had no doubt that everything east of the Sabine River would become U.S. Louisiana. "That Spanish Texas ..." he said. "Years of trouble are coming to that land, mark my words."

He and Dr. Sibley consciously avoided discussion of the idea that *that* land was obviously inhabited by *someone*, as the Orleans Territory had been.

"Madame Dupre and her son Peter Hayes," Two Hawks began, "are planning to join DeWitt's Colony. They speak of open lands, cattle for the gathering—"

"You have been there, have you not, old boy?" Sibley interrupted, smirking. "You see any of those 'free' cows?"

"Bears are free, too," Two Hawks said. "But you must stop them from killing you. I saw one cow gut a charging horse with those horns wider than a man is tall. I never thought cows were intelligent, but looking into the eyes of those things I could see hatred, a coyote eye but with a motive."

The doctor nodded, serious.

Two Hawks then related to the doctor his none too distant contact with the Karankawa he had shared with Margaret and Peter, seeing Sibley's eyes light up at the details of his friend's investigation and findings. After Two Hawks showed his friend the puckered scar where his captors had "taken a share" of the Caddo under his last rib, the doctor jotted down a sketch and description of the aloe plant the former had helped stave off infection with.

"Two Hawks, you are living too soon. Had you received more medical and scientific training, you might have discovered great things."

"Too late, doctor—we both know I am too late." The old Caddo shook his head. "Trapped as we are here between our memories and the last, well, nothing."

"But what of God, old son?"

"What a god, yes, doctor. But enough of this. There may yet be something I may accomplish—"

"Well, why not go with them, Two Hawks? You would be of great value on their journey, even when they begin to settle."

"And then I might become the tame old Indian on the back porch..."

"You are not speaking to me," said Sibley.

"And to be secure, Madame Dupre should find another husband, and he would see me as ..." Two Hawks' voice trailed off into the thicket of his musing, though it was clear to the doctor that his friend had already run down these trails and knew what lurked there, so he changed tack:

"I went to the blacksmith's yesterday," he said to Two Hawks, "to get the lock on my new fowling piece smoothed out. He told me you were having that old Charleville converted—a good idea—and he told me about some other work you had asked him to do, gave him a Spanish gold piece—don't look like that. Corey and I have known each other so many years now, but he would tell no one else ..."

Two Hawks recalled Samuel Corey's interest tempered with concern as the design of the steel arrow points the Indian had requested became clear: heavy-bodied but narrow, with four shallow blades instead of the conventional two, a shape obviously aimed at penetration of multiple layers of clothing, leather, perhaps even thin wood.

"These are man-killing points," the smith had said. "I would not want to be on the bad side of you, old man." But Corey trusted his friend's instincts and asked no questions but began forging the five points Two Hawks had requested.

Corey had tried to refuse the Spanish coin that was proffered for the work but the Indian had responded, "I have use for such things as these only to purchase what I need. I am pleased to purchase from my friends—"

"... and Peter Hays," said the doctor loudly, bringing his friend's eyes back into focus. "often gets himself into trouble just with his youth, but I expect you know that, too?"

"In former days, we Caddo travelled many days in the spring, to where the buffalo still grazed in great numbers, and we would follow alongside a herd, patient, watching like wolves to see which animals should be removed, would be best to bring down, not wanting to kill more than we needed, and the buffalo did not even know we were there—"

"You going to trail them, aren't you, Two Hawks?"

Chapter 12

The doctor still knew Two Hawks well. But first the Caddo would make a bow, perhaps his last, he thought. The season was ideal, and he had carefully selected the limb.

Resting across his knees, the blank for the bow had a natural curvature that was pleasing to the eye, appearing already bent to the string. Cut from an early spring branch of bois d'arc, Osage orange tree, the limb was almost two fingers thick and tall as a man, held onto to season at the back of the smokehouse.

Such Caddo bows, Two Hawks knew, were still prized among his people and by other tribes as well, the wood tough, hard, but resilient enough to bear the weight of those heavy lobes of green fruit at summer's end. The branch would lose two hands' length before he was finished.

His heavy trade knife, polished from use, lay in his hand, and he relished the weight of potential power, testing the edge before bringing out his Washita stone and drawing the blade in an arch back across the stone, over and over, as though trying to take thin slices of it before replacing the stone in his pouch. He leaned the wood upright against a tree and began to peel and shave, first the stubs from the outgrowth of smaller twigs, then cutting away the short thorns concealing themselves along the length. Careful not to gouge or chop, he was patient with his task, understanding that what he wrought was not simply a weapon but might one day save a life, take a life, feed and clothe, and, yes, bring a quiet pleasure to a discerning eye. He was proud of his work.

The bright yellow inner wood appeared as the upper skin of bark was shaved away, as though a light were shining from within the wood, a lightning that would strike out with the arrow, speeding it on its way. He felt power moving in his hands, into the bow. Such connections between the spirits of his world and the hard visible world always brought to the Caddo a feeling of wonder, and he thought about how few of his people spoke to him about sensing such impulses from the spirit world, other than an occasional fear of rousing bad spirits that might curse your hunt or wither your garden.

Only the shaman talked at length of communing with the spirit powers, he and the priests and missionaries telling his people about their god that somehow was really three spirits in one but none of them bad or even a trickster, and how the other god, Satan, had amazing powers but wasn't really a god, and that made no sense at all.

Not for the first time, Two Hawks wondered what he might have become had he followed a shaman's path and learned the medicine man's ways. He knew how difficult that would have been since he was not born into that caste, and Caddo did not welcome such shifting about. And he was not at all sure he would have wanted to remain in one village and work such patterned ceremonies and healing potions the people required. Besides, while he felt and knew and feared the powers of the spirits, and they did frequently speak to him through birds and bears and once even a fish, he was no longer confident that the most powerful spirits listened to and protected the Caddo.

Again he drew forth the images and ancestral memories that had washed over him upon visiting the overgrown mounds four days' walk to the west, in the lands of the Hasinai, the home of the ancient Caddo, whose powers were held tight in the huge pines that grew all around. Only that remained of a great people.

These feelings of foreboding were not new but were prodded forth by so many things around him. The heavy wood-handled knife he held between his hands to shave the bark, scraping the inner curve of the emerging bow, the hard bright steel of the blade, the endurance of the tool all argued against the lasting strength of his people. The knife had held to his side for more rounds of seasons than he had hands, the handle polished to a luster by blood and grease and sweat, by lives, but there was no sign the blade would break or wear away; instead, it mocked time and death, wood and stone, as nothing in the Caddo world could.

It was not magic; the blacksmith had shown him that as the man's heavy forearms beat out a horseshoe or a knife from the steel, softened orange-hot in the forge. He needed hammers and tongs and an anvil, true, but all of these things had come from across the water, in wondrous huge ships, and all of this had come from these Spanish and French and English who claimed their god—they all had the same one—as their power. Their god, shown suffering, nailed to wood, gave them the power and knowledge to make these things and bring them here. It was strange.

He thought again about the bow being shaped in his crooked old hands, how it would last perhaps four rounds of seasons, perhaps a few more, before the power would weaken and the weapon would serve as a deadfall trip or a stick to prod the ashes of the cook fire. So short-lived compared to his fire-starting steel or French musket—still, there was something this bow shared with his world that the steel or even the glass did not.

But on thinking of the coming seasons, Two Hawks was reasonably sure that this becoming bow in his hands would not be passed on to other uses, other years, unless accidentally happened upon. He knew this was his last bow.

Not that the temporary nature of the weapon brought him to haste or carelessness, as he believed that the care and skill one imparted into an object dwelled in it, in the luster of the pot, the soft stretch of slowly scraped and chewed leggings, the quiet spring of consistent power in a well-shaped bow. By the hands, and yes, the spirit of the maker, the artifact became an extension of the mind. He wanted to complete every step with his eye on the arrow's shaft, winging its way swifter than the drop of a falcon out of the morning sky, finding its driven rest in the fleeing spirit sent upon its way.

And thus he worked steadily, not filling each day with toil but setting aside the freshest part of the morning to turn again to his craft, smoothing and flattening the inside curve of the wood to facilitate the bend, leaving the grip in the center whole and round, gradually carving inward the arrow's rest on the left side, to be later supplemented by a section of the breastbone he had kept from a red-tailed hawk brought down whole and alive for her feathers, a crucial element in an arrow's flight. The breastbone would be held in place by a rawhide band wide as his hand, sewn in place wet, shrinking around the grip tight and hard as it dried.

That last hawk, at least this was what the Caddo believed, had come down fast and hard. Two Hawks remembered how in his younger years a red man from a people far to the west had shown him how to catch an eagle in his hands, to feel the life he was taking pass into his own body as the fierce beating of the wings slowed and were at last at rest across his arms.

And so he had gone to the sandy bluffs along the Rive Rouge to the north, trying as he often had the newer name, "Red River," in his mouth, but going back to the more liquid French "Rive Rouge" as more descriptive of the voluble currents threading between winding banks. While on some days he missed speaking entirely in Caddo, as he had when growing up, there was pleasure in picking and choosing between languages for those words that seemed to best suit the things they were attached to. "Assesino" was so much more sharp and violent than "killer" or "murderer," especially when he spoke aloud to himself.

He had chosen a part of the bluffs where run-off had dissolved the red sand-infused clay bank into a wide shaft an arm's length back and deep enough to admit a squatting man. Cottonwood branches had been cut and woven into a thick door and loose ceiling overhead, with accessible spaces between branches and leaves to admit upraised arms.

Finally prepared, he had snared a cottontail rabbit, keeping it trussed but quiet until the pre-dawn hours, when he made his way to the river.

As the day opened grey and misty along the banks, the broad green cottonwood leaves drenched with dew but still with the bitter scent of cut foliage, he entered the blind, pulling the makeshift door closed, and pulled the rabbit from beneath his deerskin shirt, where it had kept him warm with soft fur and a busy heart.

Cutting the sinew binding three of its legs, he held the rabbit's struggling form by one hind leg, welcoming its high-pitched squeaks rising into the morning air as he secured it above a central branch. Then he leaned his back on the clay wall of the blind, eyes searching intently upward, and waited, still as stone.

He watched the shadows move slowly across his folded arms as the sun rose and drifted up the cloudless sky, at intervals slowly reaching up through the leaves to prod the rabbit into movement with a thorn branch he had brought for that purpose. And he waited.

Sometime later, beginning to ready himself for relinquishing his blind until another day, the sun high and bright at midmorning, Two Hawks froze, the high-pitched calling cries of a pair of raptors piercing his ears.

Slowly rotating his face upward, he scanned the sky between the leaves, catching the broad bodies and wide wings of two red-tailed hawks wagging their feathers in adjustment to the rabbit below, the frightened animal unmoving now as it recognized the sounds of death that drew near in the blue air.

One hawk flared its wings wide and then tight to its body, and dropped like a cast-down spear, Two Hawks losing sight of its form until he felt the impact on the woven canopy above his head, the hawk clutching the rabbit in its penetrating talons.

Using his crouching legs to spring upward, Two Hawks drove both arms up through the canopy of cut branches, one hand gathering and seizing the hawk's legs above the talons buried in the rabbit's fur, the other hand shooting further up to enfold the knife-sharp beak and penetrating eye, feeling the thrashing of the great bird subside and at last rest still in his arms, the bleeding rabbit released and bouncing off his chest to the floor of the blind.

Burrowing his head up through the branches, he saw that he had been successful, the darkness of the covered eyes calming the bird, though at some cost. Two Hawks saw that the legs were firmly and safely pinned together, but in the heat of the moment he had not felt the sharp hook of the hawk's beak lay open his hand before he enclosed it, the Caddo's blood meandering down his arm in two rivulets through the sweat and broken leaves. But the flow ceased as he watched her mate circle and call up in the mid-day sky.

He quickly gathered the bird's neck into his fingers' embrace, bringing head and neck beside each other until he felt the bones and cartilage crunch, the hawk shuddering into death.

The hawk was then quickly skinned, wings cut off and folded, finally the heart removed and eaten, bitter and tough, out of respect and perhaps hope that some of her young power would guide his arrows around deflecting trees or rocks.

Later, he had made his selections of tail and wing feathers to best serve as fletching for his arrows, carefully slit along their central veins and fixed to the arrow shafts by bone glue and fine sinew in three vanes that would glide smoothly across the bone bridge when sent upon their ways.

Chapter 13

Several days after, Two Hawks began his final preparations, Margaret Dupre having given him use of a corner of her little-used storage shed behind her house to rest for a few days. He knew that she and her son would not disturb his small pile of covered travelling kit. The bow he gave a final smoothing with sand on the creek nearby and thoroughly rubbed the wood down with the contents of a blackened pouch, the remaining globules of fat from the tail of an otter he had found dead in a beaver trap, the otter's dense yellow fat darkening the bright bare wood of the bow and imparting a strong enough scent to mask his own.

"Madame, you are going on this journey? Your mind is convinced?" Two Hawks began that evening.

"Old friend, the house is sold. The new owners will take possession next week. Peter and I have loaded the wagons, and we depart with the others for San Augustine tomorrow. I do wish you would consider again and come with us. We could all begin a new life, with promise and—"

"Ah," the Caddo said, and inwardly smiled at his acquisition of old Blue Heron's mannerism. "My one life is enough and my path lies elsewhere. Peter Hays—"

"Yes, old one?" Peter shot back. He was more than a little peeved at the old Indian for coming back into their lives and then stubbornly refusing to continue with them. Peter was also more than a bit frightened of the long journey that lay ahead, knowing that he would be responsible for his mother's safety and the safety of their possessions. While confident, perhaps unreasonably so, that he was capable of handling daily situations in Natchitoches, that long unknown road was daunting, and he had always felt, well, secure whenever the old man had been around. "If you will not come with us, what have you to say?"

"Bon chance, Mr. Hays," Two Hawks said, in a formal tone and expression. "Your mother will rely on your strength and wisdom."

Margaret Dupre saw her son stand a bit straighter, taller, buoyed by the old Caddo, who added, "The road is long and perhaps dangerous, but much of the way was once Caddo land, and that spirit may still watch over you."

"We'll need more than old Indian spirits," Peter said, and went back into the house for another bundle to load into the wagon.

When he came out, Two Hawks was gone. "Where did he go, Mother?"

"Oh, you know him, Peter. He looked quite seriously at me, took my hand and bowed over it as if he were going to kiss it like some French count, and then quietly strode away."

"But," said Peter, "I wanted—"

"As did I, son."

Early the following morning, six wagons, several pulled by two mules each, two by powerful draught horses, preceded and followed by six outriders on horseback, made their way west out of town toward the Sabine River, toward, they all anticipated, new lives. They expected to be met in Nacogdoches by a number of others to comprise the initial contingent of DeWitt's Colony.

While the wagon beds were not sprung, and thus transmitted each rut and rock to the passengers, this part of the road, the old Camino Real, had already been in virtually constant use for more than a century and had been smoothed out to an almost paved consistency, at least when dry.

"Where do you suppose old Two Hawks has gone, Mother? Where does he go? Do you suppose he has some Indian cabin far away in the woods somewhere?"

"Peter, he has never told me much about his private life, at least not about his personal habitations, but I do not think he has a home other than where he stands. He has had a sad life, and he is a fine man, and it brings me to tears to see the understanding in his eyes, that fine a man as he is, and good as he is, and he is a good man, Peter, that he is an example of the best his people can do ... but the best must simply disappear, simply not exist."

"But there are Indians everywhere, more Indians where we are going—Caddo, Tonkawa, Karankawa, perhaps even Comanche and some called Lipans, from what I hear. Mother, there will always be Indians."

"Peter, have you ever seen a wolf?"

"I have heard one ..."

"Are you sure?"

"Well, no, but I'm pretty sure it was."

"And how many bears have you seen? How many have you gotten close to?"

"Well, I helped dress out that big black bear Nathan shot down in the bayou bottom that time—Lord, that thing stank. There are great numbers of bears when we get away from town."

"But, son, soon there will not be any more bears, just like there are not any more wolves. And our old friend knows, just like one day there will not be any more Caddoes, at least not around here. What happens when we come to our land and we want to plant cotton and grow hay and raise cattle? What will we do? What must we do?"

"Well, we have to clear our land, cut the trees, build a house and plant the crops—I know how to do these things, Mother. I will work hard. You'll see."

"Yes, I will see, Peter, and I believe you, and you will be a good man, a fine man. But the Caddo, even our friend Two Hawks, they are like the trees. Fine as they may be, he knows and I know that they will be, they must be ... removed."

"So, Mother, when I am clearing our land, that is what we are doing to the Caddoes? You think that?" Peter was not pleased with the direction this discussion was going in, and his vision was clouded by that understanding.

"But, son, there is nothing to be done. The wheels of time continue to revolve, and grind like millstone whatever lies in their path. Do you not think that you and I and Two Hawks might not be happy to live together and create a home and a future?"

"Well, I never thought—"

"Not in this life, Peter, not in this world and this time," Margaret said, and, eyes brimming, looked off into the thick forest that lined the road.

"Come on, you old cow," Peter said. His mother was surprised by the harsh words, but then she saw him slap the mule's back with the reins, "Get up there—hey!" He half-stood and jerked back on the harness as the right-hand mule craned her neck down to grab a bunch of grass from the side of the road. "You can eat when we do—tonight—you old jenny. Get on!" He shouted and slapped the reins again until she dragged her head about, gave half a hop, and resumed a brisk walk.

"Mother, I have had half a mind that what Two Hawks said to us yesterday meant that he was going to follow us somehow, because, I don't know, I have felt something out there, something along with us, but I don't feel good about it, not like it's Two Hawks, but that it is waiting ..."

"I have felt it, too, Peter, but perhaps we are simply frightened at the, well, open-ended feeling, at the insecurity of what we are doing. But we *will* make a new life, a better life, you will see."

"The colony's lands are described as promising ... but look there, Mother—there, next to that big tree with the broken branch—a face, a top knot, just for an instant and it was gone."

"I see nothing, Peter. Are you certain? Our imaginations are so excited by what we have not seen—"

"No, it was a person, an Indian, but young. I saw him only for a moment, but I would recognize him now, as though he wanted me to see him, wanted me to know he was out there—"

"But how did he look? Was he friendly?"

"Not friendly, not exactly menacing, maybe my age or a few years older, long straight tattoos on his cheeks, three of them I think, and, well, he just looked *intent*."

"Probably just a young Caddo out on a hunt."

"In the middle of the day?"

"There may be a larger hunting group, or a garden nearby ..."

"Well, I will keep my eyes open—hand me that fouling piece Dr. Sibley gave us, please, and I'll lean it against that sack of meal."

"I'll miss the good doctor. He didn't need a new gun, not at his age. I think he bought it just so he could give us his old one for the move."

As the line of wagons moved west and south, passing fewer and fewer settlers' cabins, the road became more rutted and stony, the click of hooves on rock outcroppings and sounds of settling crates and creaking sideboards from the jostled wagons often were all that was heard in the bright spring day. Most of the prospective colonists rode in contemplation of what lay ahead, and they planned their homes, designed the barns, imagined quiet pastures dotted with grazing cattle, knowing that much of this lay many years ahead.

On several occasions as the day wore on, Peter handed the reins to his mother on a long, relatively straight stretch of trail, got down and stealthily moved up on a clump of roadside brush where he had earlier seen a rabbit run and conceal itself as a lead wagon neared. Twice he found the animal crouching, still, attempting to find safety in immobility, and he dispatched the animal with a quick blow to the head, delivered by the arm's length hickory stick Two Hawks had made him years earlier, the limber stick ending with a peach-sized stone sweated in place with shrunken rawhide.

When he was younger, Peter had spent many hours in the woods with the old Caddo, learning the patience and stealth that made him a productive hunter, coming to understand that two rabbits for tonight were much more satisfying for others who depended upon you, than the deer that bolted an instant before your shot found it.

They made camp an hour before the sunset, in a makeshift clearing near Spotted Woman Creek, ensuring that they would have more than enough time to gather wood, build fires, water the animals, and prepare adequate sleeping quarters before darkness closed in, and with it the scavengers, both four and two-legged, that may draw close.

And since this was their first encampment of many to come, even though they had thought over the procedures with care, the first night out was always a time of discovery and adjustment.

This first meal of the journey, other than a *petite dejeuner* of cured ham, hard-boiled eggs and hard bread Margaret and Peter had shared earlier in the day, was much simpler than those of the days and the weeks to come. After collecting sufficient deadwood to provide a cook fire that would serve not only for the evening but for the breakfast as well, Peter built the fire, set up the iron cross-bar, and took the rabbits down to the creek to skin and clean, having gutted them earlier along the road.

Margaret had hung the cast-iron pot from the crossbar over the fire to heat, adding some scraps of ham fat rescued from their earlier meal to grease the bottom. The skinned rabbits were added to the popping fat to brown, their carcasses packed with wild onion and a pinch of coarse salt. She then added a chopped tomato, garden onion, and half a handful of parched native pecan meats, along with some small but fiery cayenne peppers, letting the mix brown for some minutes before de-glazing with a cup or two of molasses-infused creek water.

As the fire dropped down to glowing coals, so, too, the stew simmered lower and lower as she and her son constructed an oil-skin tarpaulin lean-to stretched from the top edge of the main wagon-bed to the ground, affording sufficient protection from the falling dew and the constant threat of a passing shower. The bedding was then laid out but not unrolled until they were ready for sleep (no reason to invite a roaming snake or scorpion or blister beetle).

The china carefully packed away in a wooden crate, the two ate quickly from deep tin plates, the steaming rabbit falling off the delicate bones and the spicy sauce and onions pooling in a pile of leftover grits warmed up in a stoneware dish set on a stone next to the fire to warm.

The second rabbit, now preserved in the rich sauce, would supply tomorrow's supper as well.

Tea was served in thick stoneware cups, Madame having made more than enough to be re-heated in the morning to save time or allow for a quick camp-breaking, though she had little concern of sleeping past others' rousing. The sun had rarely surprised Margaret Dupre.

The spring darkness took its time in enveloping the encampment, sounds of stowing dinner utensils and shifting cargoes gradually giving way to the nocturnal forest birds and the occasional rustle of waddling scavengers. Margaret had left the stewpot over the fire, further weighing the top with a stone to dissuade the prying black hands of the ever-present camp bandits, the raccoons.

Unlike several other settlers, Margaret and Peter did not waste tallow or candle wax after the meal but immediately turned in after cleaning the dishes, lying under the tarp, the ground softened by several layers of wool blankets. The humid evening removed any need for a cover, though both mother and son lay under their muslin sheets to ward off at least some of the humming mosquitoes waiting in the still air, the two lost in their own thoughts, waiting for sleep.

Chapter 14

Margaret had woken numerous times during the night, at times by confusing and fearful dreams (one in which Two Hawks had stolen her Peter and was carving hideous tattoos on her son's face), but at other times when she had heard some small animal rummaging through the camp. She suspected that her restless night was part the exposure to foreign environment, partly the heightened awareness that she believed came with having children. Clearly recalling when one of her children simply turning over or coughing or when a creaking board or scurrying mouse would snap her eyes wide open at three o'clock in the morning, she awoke just as the east was beginning to grey with false dawn, resigned to the understanding that she did not outgrow maternity.

The coals deeply buried in last night's ash soon caught the kindling she had collected by rolling together dry leaves and moss with some of her still dark brown hair she had pulled from her brush; a new succession of twigs and the heavier branches caught and began to warm the tea kettle, Peter rising and rubbing the sleep from his eyes.

"Good morning, son. We'll have the last of those grits before we load up."

He stretched and shook out his bedding, draping it over the wagon wheel to dry some of the ground moisture. "I'll go see about the mules and horses," Peter said. He didn't want to admit to a restless night as well, lest the admission be heard as fear. He walked toward the picketed animals, quickly pulling up his shirt and dropping his trousers as soon as he was shielded by the trees, urinating but also carefully feeling for lice or wood ticks that might have found a home during the night.

"Peter, did you become hungry during the night?" Margaret said, when he returned with the mules in tow.

"I'm always hungry," Peter said. "Why do you ask?"

"I wanted to save that second rabbit for this evening's supper—"

"I know that—you explained that last night—I have not eaten any!"

"Well, that is strange," she said. "I moved the stewpot from the fire this morning, removed the stone weighing down the lid, and saw that one of the rabbit's haunches had been cleanly cut off."

"Perhaps a coon, Mother—you know how clever they can be—"

"But I have never known one to replace a lid, much less the stone holding it down."

They both began mentally cataloging and trying to evaluate the sounds that had awoken them during the night but could not clearly identify one that might suggest an answer.

"Two Hawks," Peter said. "The old boy is following us and snuck in for a bite of rabbit last night—"

"No, Peter. He could do it but would not, not without leaving us a clear sign."

"Whatever it is," Peter said, "wanted us to know they are out there."

"Wanted us to know they could come in while we slept," she added. "I do not like mysteries. But—enough. Get the mules in harness, son, so the others will not need to wait for us."

And so for a time they drove away thoughts of who might be in the trees. Camp was quickly broken and stowed for another day, the first mile of road asplash with the animals' morning waste of bright green digested grass as they found their gait and settled into the day's labor.

Three miles ahead, well back from the Camino Real track, Two Hawks had covered his musket and packs under a bush, finding the low-draping limbs of a huge old oak resting on the ground easy enough for his old arms and legs to climb, soon three man-heights above the forest floor, and he settled in to wait, realizing long ago that very few humans or animals bothered to scan the upper reaches. Other than a very desperate cougar, there was little for a sizable animal to fear from above.

He heard the click and crunch of the wagons, the calls of the hostlers, long before he saw them. A cluster of deer trotted through the underbrush ahead of the sounds, a massive old buck shepherding his gaggle of does, two of them already heavy with developing offspring. Two men were walking their horses ahead of the wagons, leaning in their saddles toward each other to engage in quiet conversation.

The Caddo's watchful old eyes caught a subtle movement underneath his perch as, unaware of his position, a lone individual ghosted through the underbrush ahead but parallel to the wagons' passage.

Again blessing the spirits and his long-departed parents for his still-keen eyesight, Two Hawks slid around the large limb of the oak out of sight amongst the feathering ferns and drape of moss, to gather a full read of the man when he turned to look back over his trail.

A young Indian, not yet fully a grown man, the stalker had the old-fashioned topknot and full tattoos of the Caddo, including what appeared to be three angled black claw marks on each cheek. And while he wore the breechclout and moccasins of the Indian, he was clad in a French shirt soil-rubbed for camouflage and carried a relatively new powder horn and shorter version of the Brown Bess musket converted to percussion. Overall, the young brave, like a ferret, gave off the heat and intensity of the hunt.

Growing concerned, Two Hawks questioned whether this apparent Caddo was alone or the scout for a larger party. He was well aware that the Neutral Ground was rife with outlaws, renegades, and runaway slaves, being a land of opportunity for those not longing for the comforts of government authority. Established years earlier by the mutual agreements of the Mexican and U.S. governments, this area between the Sabine and Calcaseau Rivers was still virtually lawless.

While he was somewhat ashamed of the Caddo renegades and felt no inclination to participate, Two Hawks understood, even sympathized with their choice. Having so often been tricked, abused, and disregarded by so many of the Anglo settlers, traders, and hangers on, including the blind eyes of their white governments, some had chosen to turn equally lawless and ruthless, if not more so, and prey upon the people who had increasingly marginalized or made virtually impossible the traditional Caddo way of life. The renegades were doomed eventually to the rifle or the rope, but Two Hawks sometimes wondered if those were not preferable to the slow and pathetic, and in the end inevitable, decay of the tribes who kept the ways of peace.

Nonetheless, while he might be more than willing to walk away from an Indian attack on village or wagon, Two Hawks felt drawn to intervene if the safety of Margaret and Peter were in question, and he did not entirely understand why. He had befriended them, even before Monsieur Hays and Dupre had died, and he had invested time in teaching the boy the crafts and both of them many of the stories of the Caddo. And they had returned that friendship, always with open respect and affection, but he was not, after all, their family.

But continuance, perhaps in some strange way it had to do with continuance, or value. While all of his family, parents, his beloved wife and two very young children were long dead and forgotten by all but an isolated old man, had they lived, were any of them still alive—Two Hawks regretfully admitted, while feeling guilty as well, that he would not wish any of them to be alive, to grow to maturity and then age in this time when there was neither happiness nor future for the Caddo. He would not wish that world to be theirs.

And here the mystery deepened for him. As through some transmission or metamorphosis, Margaret and Peter sometimes felt, had always felt, like his own family in new skins, as though had his family been reborn into a form that had a future, they would have been like Margaret and Peter. He never thought this unfaithful to his Caddo family memory but instead a way that who his wife and children would have been, and who he was, would be carried on, continued.

And perhaps this was just the foolish musing of an emotional old man, he thought, since other than a few other old men like the doctor and a few traders and old strays he suspected were still alive here in the wild, Margaret and Peter were the best of whom still knew him in this world.

No matter, he concluded. He always felt most alive with a bone in his teeth, and this journey was beginning to develop an edge. That quiver of steel-tipped bees waiting for him under the leaves, with his bow and musket, might have been more foresight than vanity.

Two Hawks crab-walked down the broad limb some time after his mysterious traveler and the wagons had passed, having tried to mentally send a warning to Margaret and Peter, who had both been lost in thought as their wagon had rolled by, eyes downcast. He made up his mind to gather more information about the young Caddo, "renegade" he would have to call the young man, perhaps visit his evening camp. With increased care and attention to stray sounds or movement, knowing well that a good hunter might well circle back, Two Hawks gathered his gear, stringing his bow across his back but keeping his musket loaded in his right hand, half-cocked and a percussion cap in place. Speed might be crucial in the event of a surprise, and he might not have time to nock an arrow and draw back his bow.

While these preparations were taking place, he clearly remembered the old bear that had brought the lesson to his home, and in a number of ways had brought him to this ground and moment.

Chapter 15

Two Hawks had been in the prime of his young manhood. Gold Feather, his wife, cared for their dwelling and two young children with a quiet grace and cheer that gladdened his heart whenever his eyes rested upon her form or heard the burbling laughter of his children like as stream sounding over stones. That time between late spring and early summer, it had been, in their village not too distant from the Sabine River but north of his present location. The gardens were lush with bean plants and corn stalks, the peppers already beginning to produce shiny pods all in a uniform green color at this point. The rains had swept up from the big water with a nourishing regularity, and even the deer seemed to wander near his drawn bow in willing sacrifice.

Swelling quickly in the balance rain and sunshine, blackberries and dewberries ripened early that season, and Gold Feather, with her son, Otter, and daughter, Magnolia Flower, had gone, two delicately woven grass baskets in hand, to the dense thorny patches of berries down near Crazy Woman Creek, also armed with a long forked stick and child-sized club. Everyone knew that snakes, particularly rattlesnakes and those lazy fat copperheads, frequently lay loosely coiled under the blackberry canes, waiting for berry-hungry birds to forget themselves in the feast.

In a very short time, finding no reptiles to slow their harvest, Gold Feather had filled both baskets, receiving some help from the children, though their ruby-smeared faces and hands were clear indications where most of their pickings had gone. She knew, too, that their bee-hive shaped home would be alive with their complaints as their thorn scratches crusted and healed.

No one had heard the bear approach.

The old black bear had not been in a benevolent mood. Two weeks earlier he had been tearing open a deeply rotted tupelo trunk that had been uprooted years ago in a spring tornado, the damp inner wood exposed and alive with the sweet grubs he quickly licked out and relished. Distracted, he had not heard the approach of the young Spanish hunter, flintlock loaded and primed.

And to his credit, the hunter had stalked close enough to feel comfortable aiming for a neck shot, but in the moment between the fall of the flint-armed hammer and the flash of gunpowder in the pan that sent a spark through the touch hole to ignite the shot load, the old bear heard the foreign sound and began to raise his huge old head and turn in the direction of the sound. The ball chipped the bone in his foreleg and lodged close to the surface of the skin on the inner side.

Roaring in pain and confusion, the black bear had lurched, reared himself briefly on his hind legs, and broke into a shambling run, crashing through the brush, the shock of the traumatized flesh keeping the pain at bay for a time.

Over the next several days, Two Hawks later surmised, the musket ball had been pulled about just under the thick skin of the bear's right foreleg, that and the growing soreness of the bullet's infected track causing the bear to severely limp, and his usual prey of a stumbling fawn or even a litter of unearthed fox kits had been beyond consideration. Reduced to licking up what ants and grubs he could find, and the eggs from an occasional low bird's nest, soon the old bear had begun to slowly starve, his brain maddened by the spreading pain.

The bear had probably smelled the blackberries crushed into the mouths of the children before he had seen them. Later, going back over the tracks, Two Hawks noted that the animal had approached from downwind, the scent of food overcoming that hateful human smell also carried on the breeze.

What happened had been relatively simple for the Caddo to reconstruct. Returning from a dawn-break deer hunt, a meaty but barren doe carried across his shoulders, Two Hawks soon had found out from the old woman who stayed in the dwelling next to his, her eyes almost completely obscured by cataracts, that his family had gone to the further creek, berry picking. In the early afternoon, growing concerned by their lengthy absence, the young father had gone to investigate.

The blackberry canes had been visible from a distance, and as he hurried forward, the torn-up forest litter and the frightening silence had begun to speak of a violent encounter. The smells of bowels emptied in fear and the coppery tang of fresh blood rolled over him at the same time that he saw the bodies.

Gold Feather's neck had been bitten almost through, her abdomen gutted, probably by a single swipe of the bear's paw.

Two Hawks had collapsed into a sitting position, his back against a tree, stunned by the enormity of what had obviously happened.

Some minutes later, he had struggled to his feet, eyes filmed over by the soundless weeping of loss, and soon found the children, Otter's head bearing the four crushed holes of the bear's canines as the boy's skull had been squeezed by the bear's powerful jaws—at least he would have died almost instantly before the beast had flung the body against a small oak.

Magnolia Flower, half covered under what appeared to be a hasty attempt to conceal the child, had been bitten through at the shoulder, her left leg torn from its socket, perhaps consumed.

The bear's tracks were everywhere, showing that he had approached and reared onto his hind legs before breaking into a very awkward charge and beginning his rampage. Signs of the violent rage that had overtaken the animal had rent the earth and brush, as well as the bodies he had left behind.

Two Hawks' village had responded quickly to the news, several men following him back to the scene and then carrying the broken bodies, his broken dreams, back for burial. He himself had held Gold Feather in his arms on the walk back to his dwelling, her blood soaking through the seams of his deerskin shirt. He had felt nothing of that, only the growing thirst for punishment, the drive to find and kill the bear that had killed so much of him.

The elders had convinced the young Two Hawks to see his family buried before he set out on the hunt, and he was now mildly surprised that he recalled almost nothing of the burial ceremonies or even his tracking of the bear, a work he had insisted on accomplishing alone, not wanting to share his revenge or potential failure, though he had little concern that he would fail.

The bear had taken shelter for the night under a clay cut bank on a small creek a day's travel west of the village, his lair partially shrouded by tree roots of the higher forest floor reached by the high water's flow. Two Hawks had climbed up into a tree some distance away to pass the night and take the bear when it rose in the morning, the Indian confused at the animal's repeated moanings and series of growls brought to his ears through the night air. The hateful bear must be beset by demon spirits, he had thought, and drifted into a tired sleep.

Later, in the early dawn, immediately apparent had been the bear's seriously injured forepaw and his constant agony as he had struggled out from under the roots. At the first sign of the animal's distraction by his pain, Two Hawks had quietly slid down the trunk of his tree on the side away from the bear, nocked an arrow and moved forward, ready to loose his first arrow at any moment, but wishing to get as close as possible for an accurate placement.

The Caddo's movement at last catching the old bear's exhausted eyes, he rose on his hind legs and roared out his outrage at being thus challenged so soon from his bed, though in looking back Two Hawks thought the bear's rage was not only at this Indian that dared confront him but at this world that had seemed in his declining years to so have turned against him.

The first arrow took the bear full on at the base of his throat, careening off his vertebrae and burrowing through to almost half its length. The bear just stood, confused, dropped both forepaws and looked at Two Hawks.

The second arrow pierced the bear just below where Two Hawks had guessed the rib cage to end, again going in to half its length. And then the man was amazed to see the huge old black bear look almost askance at his attacker as he had first sat back on his haunches and then simply fell over on his side with a groan that was almost human.

As he cautiously approached the still form of the bear, Two Hawks immediately saw the suppurating wound licked bare of the thick fur of the foreleg. He probed the entrance hole, then pulling the massive old leg up, noting a swelling on the other side. His knife then exposed the .69 caliber ball, which popped out into his hand on squeezing. Furious, disappointed, Two Hawks sat back onto the mat of pine needles next to the carcass, looking over into the dead bear's glazed eyes, hung slightly open in death, thick tracks of rheum marking either side of the great muzzle, an indication of the near-constant pain his leg and the ensuing infection had caused.

And the anger and frustration and sadness all warred across the Caddo's features, this pathetic arena swimming through his tears.

No one's fault, Two Hawks had thought, nothing's fault—nothing to blame or beat or kill or satisfy himself with—not the hunter or the bear or even himself for being away on a hunt of his own, surely not his woman or children for wanting blackberries. Just this ugly earth or the restless spirits that had arranged the doomed players of this final dance, the unseen tricksters the shaman always tried to outwit.

A female cardinal had fluttered up to the low branch of a pine sapling not three strides away, the broken sunlight playing on the soft doeskin feathers and lighting up her bill, the orange of a sunset. She looked this way and that, a fat tender caterpillar still wriggling in her beak, no doubt destined for her hatched and hungry brood.

And he had opened his mouth, almost in a curse on such a world where her babies lived and his entire family had fallen prey to the temper of a sick bear, but he could not. The bird was beautiful, and so was the play of sunlight through the pine needles, and much as he hated to admit it, so was this stinking old bear. He was as confused by his own reaction as he was by this disastrous turn of events.

Chapter 16

So now what? Two Hawks had thought, and sat next to the bear as the flies settled in to begin their transformations. As he took stock of himself and his world, almost, inwardly finding some irony, like Abraham Colley checking over his wares as Two Hawks had seen him do at the trading post, there was no doubt that try as he might he loved this world, how it looked and worked and was. Also, not for the first time he was amazed at how swiftly his emotions had been overruled and directed by the workings of his logical mind. He saw, sometimes after a collection of materials or sense impressions, how things fit together inexorably into an answer, a truth that was something he had built as surely as another chose to construct a bowl or a bow.

And Two Hawks had known as soon as he thought about it that he relished the process of his mind, as things fell into place, like that clean sharp click of half-cock then back into full-cock of the musket's hammer, and the slow tug of the trigger before the hammer drove forward to make the shot. He had learned, himself, to be a weapon.

The realization had been both disconcerting and resolving. Never again would he relinquish hostages to the whims of this earth, or so he had thought, and thus he would remain alone, but he had known that to be constant to what he was, he would resolve himself to be a solver, Caddo, yes, always Caddo, but ultimately and forever a truth tracker, an answer stalker, even if the ultimate prey was ugly and disappointing. Because after all, he had decided that the constant that he himself was ultimately had become a rare permanence in this ever shifting, and recently at least, ever losing earth.

But that self-revelation had been many, many seasons ago, and much had indeed changed and been lost. Two Hawks reached back over his shoulder to make sure his quiver and arrows remained accessible to hand, and he let out an involuntary groan, feeling again that dull heavy pain, not always, not when he picked something up or even when he brought a weight forward toward his head or chest. The pain, where his arm was joined to his torso, would strike when he lifted his right arm up to the side or, as now, when he reached overhead or behind and pulled. It had gotten very slowly and gradually worse over the past four seasons—he hoped it would not intrude on this current purpose.

While picking up and resettling his packs and pouches gathered from under the leaves, he began pacing after the wagons' mysterious follower. Two Hawks moved very carefully that day, remaining vigilant in his attempt to discover where the other Indian might make his camp that night. The elder Caddo would learn much from this.

However, as evening approached and the wagonmasters began pulling into a rough clearing near a stand of cypress along another stream bed, clicking to the mules as the younger men and boys unharnessed the mules, the younger Caddo in the French shirt, now a considerable distance ahead and away from the group of wagons, looked about only briefly before dropping his belongings at the needle-cushioned base of a towering pine almost as thick as a man is tall and leaned his musket against the bark, squatting with his back alongside the barrel.

Two Hawks found a substantial tree and, on the side of the trunk away from the other man, climbed up into the branches, selecting a limb that would hold him from sight for the night. He noted that the other man had no intention of building a fire or a shelter of any kind but, like Two Hawks himself, was determined to pass the night with as little fuss or disturbance as possible.

A sliver of moon rose steadily through the streaming clouds as, the dew having fallen and the whites' encampment long in their blankets and their animals asleep on their tired feet, the younger Indian rose and stretched as if preparing to depart.

Two Hawks raised his head from a moss cushion and flexed his stiff old fingers but saw that the other man had begun stepping purposefully toward the roadside encampment, leaving his belongings where they lay.

Considering the opportunity to search the other man's abandoned pouches and weapon, Two Hawks instead set out in quiet pursuit, concerned that the one he followed might choose this night as the time to cause serious harm to the sleeping travelers.

Instead, the nocturnal visitor, delicately placing each step, made his way past the sleeping forms of two of the drivers and, Two Hawks tensing apprehensively, approached the fire by which Margaret and Peter's still forms lay encased in their muslin shrouds under the lean-to. He leaned across the dull embers of their evening cook fire, lifting the stone Margaret had placed on the stew pot's cast-iron lid, lifting the lid and fishing out several large pieces of smoked dried beef that had been stewed with peppers and onions into a softer consistency. He quickly ate most but left one on top of the lid, next to the replaced stone.

He obviously wants them to know there has been an intruder, Two Hawks thought, but the man's purpose remained inscrutable. And his brief nocturnal visit had not provided time enough for the older man to search the other's kit unobserved.

The following day, early morning, camp had been broken and the wagons had begun to roll. Two Hawks had stowed his gear and worked his way through a plum-sized clump of pemmican, thinking over his strategy for following his adopted family as well as learning more about the Caddo youth. His tree bunk had left his old joints a bit cramped and sore, but his irritation soon grew upon discovering that the other man had vanished. Perhaps he was getting too old for this.

Assuming that the young man had moved on ahead, Two Hawks resolved to look and step carefully so as not to overtake the man too quickly and reveal himself. Again compressing his lips in impatience at the incontinence of his age, he was leaning against the trunk of a sapling oak in a sunlit clearing opened in the forest by a tornado touching down, urinating for the third time within half the morning.

The sharp blow to the back of his head brought darkness.

Chapter 17

"Open your eyes, old man," Two Hawks heard from what seemed inside of a cave, but the strong smell and splash of liquid brought him more clearly into consciousness, realizing that the man he trailed had indeed circled back to overtake him and was now urinating on the older man's face.

Intention became instantly clear—the man meant serious harm, death, to have confronted the elder Caddo in such a manner, though the elder man resolved to feign less attention than he in fact maintained. He unobtrusively tested the bonds on his wrists behind him and curiously felt his legs bound at ankle and just above the knees, both of his feet resting on a flat piece of sandstone, another stone under his legs at midlength.

"Open your eyes, old man Two Hawks—I know you are alert now, and I want to look into your eyes when I tell you what I will do."

Two Hawks glanced up, surprised by the dispassionate hatred in the man's tone, and by eyes that glittered like broken bottle glass. "I am sad to see such bitter resolve in a man so young," he said.

"Oh, I will bring you to more than sadness, righteous one. My mother, who suckled me on revenge since the day I was born, alone and outlawed in a riverbank hole. You remember my mother—you killed her twice—"

"I have never killed a woman—"

The young man kicked Two Hawks sharply just below the ribcage. "Liar! You killed her when you falsely accused her of shooting her beloved husband."

No. Two Hawks thought, this cannot be.

"And you killed her again, stabbed her, in Natchitoches years ago."

"Your mother's name cannot be She-de-ah—"

"Oh, but it is—not was, though her body is gone. She lives on in me and will until I, Snake, lay her spirit to rest in her vengeance."

"I do not know what she told you, young one, but she killed her husband and took her own life trying to get me hanged. She had no children she told me—"

"She lied to you, old man, so you would not look over your shoulder. Yes, I was born in that hole but there was no bear to eat the baby—she used to laugh about that, knowing you would of course believe another bear story. Many remember the story of your family."

"Then you ...?"

"I was raised to hate you, to expect your lies about my mother, to take your family a second time—"

69

"I have no family left, boy. I am all there is."

"You think I am stupid? I have been watching you, listening about you for *years*. I know why you are on this trail—*whites!* Well, you would watch over those two—"

"I don't understand ..."

"Then understand this, old man," Snake said, suddenly raising his right foot higher than his waist and bringing it down sharply on Two Hawks' shin raised between the two rocks. Both bones in the lower half of older man's right leg snapped like a pistol shot, and he screamed at the pain.

"I could have killed you many times, Caddo Two Hawks, and you will live—I trust your abilities—but know this: by the time you are able to catch up with your beloved Margaret and Peter—yes, I know them well—I will have made them pay for you before I cut their throats and watch them die. I have practiced all my short life for this time."

"You—" Two Hawks choked on the pain he felt in shifting his legs.

But Snake had merely chortled, turned and walked away. And the dispassionate calm that had settled over the young man disturbed Two Hawks through the physical pain he felt.

The remainder of the morning Two Hawks spent removing his bindings, the wrists relatively easy but removing the leg bindings was punctuated by groans of pain and perspiring rests when the broken bone ends grated. He felt over his lower leg, not pleased to find that the bones overlapped at the breaks, knowing then a simple splint would not suffice.

Casting about for wood that might serve as reasonable braces once the bones were set, he found only soft pine and cracked oak branches in the immediate vicinity, but then he pulled himself over to where his equipment had been cast aside but left entire: unsheathing his heavy knife, he cut away the rawhide grip of his beloved bois d'arc bow and began hacking methodically at the thick middle, until the long bow lay in two pieces, stiff but flexible,, and with a gentle curve that would suit his purpose. He did not look forward to the next stage.

Sweating profusely with the pain, he hobbled, using a makeshift deadwood crutch, out of the clearing and to the base of a young broadleaf oak, tied the bow splints together next to his broken leg and, arm over arm, pushing upward with his healthy leg, made his way up the trunk of the tree until he was well over his own height.

Selecting a forked branch that would hold his weight, he maneuvered parallel to the ground, tying the ankle of his injured leg tightly into the fork. He understood the danger of losing consciousness inverted too long, which brought back a fond memory of making a fire with Caddo children seasons ago, but pushed that thought away.

Feeling the ankle firmly in the fork, Two Hawks leaned forward and dropped into a vertical hang by his broken leg, the pain quickly shrouding his mind in sparks and then darkness.

Coming to, his head throbbing from the suffusion of blood, he noticed from the angle of the sun on his arm that very little time had passed, and he reached up to an adjacent limb and began a hand over hand crawl upward and along the limb that held his injured leg, using the other leg for leverage. Sliding himself backward until he sat up on the limb with his back against the main trunk, both legs stretched out before him, Two Hawks bent at the waist as far as he was able, not nearly as far as he had been able in his youth, he noted.

The attached halves of his bow were then strapped tightly along his set calf, tears squeezed from his eyes at the pain.

By mid-afternoon, Two Hawks was hobbling on his way, musket over his left shoulder and a stout green oak-branch crutch under his right arm, thinking as he went that he had at least several days to catch the wagons, and Snake.

Putting himself into the mind of his antagonist, he judged that the young brave (and the boy was a warrior, he had to give him that, misguided and misled as he was) would assume that the old man would take at least a full day to recover and another several to find a means of pursuit. Snake would want to prolong his revenge, now that it was apparently in hand.

Two Hawks had to prove his opponent wrong by moving and mending faster than the other thought possible—surprise, certainly not strength, would be his only advantage.

And while he drove himself on with a ferocity that was alien but necessary for success, all the same over the coming days Two Hawks would feel a growing frustration at having to kill the boy to stop him, at having to take yet another life, the life of a young man in his prime who had based his purposes on mistaken beliefs, on the lies of a woman who had needed to hurt someone for her hurt.

Two Hawks' more immediate needs were of course food and water, though at this time of the year the rains kept every stream running. He still had a small supply of pemmican and jerked beef but needed to save those reserves in the event that an extended watch or immobility prevented his finding other sources.

Toward evening, gathering some dewberries to bait bird snares, he heard an answer in the distinct dry buzzing of a rattlesnake. Two Hawks usually left those creatures to their own designs, but the hefty diamondback he saw coiled a man's length away represented two days of meat, so the Caddo very slowly balanced on his left leg, reversed his crutch and pushing forward pinned the snake's head in the fork of the crutch but falling forward on the writhing form, trying hard to avoid letting his pain distract his focus. He grabbed the snake just behind the swollen jaws, bringing out his knife to sever the head and cast it far into the underbrush, knowing of more than one careless woodsman to have been bitten by a detached head.

The gutted form continued to writhe, headless in the leaves for some time, and two partly digested field mice in the stomach were discarded, being of no value.

Chapter 18

Knowing that his quarry must have camped miles ahead near the wagons, Two Hawks risked a fire on a sandbank of a large active creek as the sun went down. He knew he needed nourishment and rest if he were to catch up in the few days he probably had left, so he built the fire until the consuming flames were tall and brightest as the sun moved below the horizon, piling the glowing coals as darkness descended. Finally he loosely tied the rattlesnake into a knot and laid it over the embers to cook and steam in its own skin, though he could not resist stuffing the belly slit with a crushed juniper branch he had gathered for that purpose along the way.

The steam of escaping moisture died away after some time, and he saw with satisfaction that the tender coil began to break open of its own accord as he dragged it out of the heat.

The flesh, white and shiny in the moonlight, was sweet and clean-tasting; having obviously fed on small woodland creatures instead of waterfowl, the snake had no hint of the fish taste of alligator and cottonmouth. Two Hawks ate his fill, leaning back against the trunk of a drifted tree trunk and looking up at the swarm of stars in wonder and not a little fear, trying to understand why the spirits of this earth were demanding so much of him. With compressed lips but no answers, he tucked the remainder in wild grape leaves before enfolding them into a pouch that he then suspended from a branch as food for the following day. Sleep came quickly to him, his legs stretched out, pain in his splinted leg waking him only a few times during the night.

Waking in the early morning light feeling refreshed, even restored, he rose and the blood ran to his broken leg, his groans silencing complaining blue jays in a tree nearby. Working the stiffness out in loading himself with his kit took more time than he would have liked, but he was soon step-clomping with alacrity toward the west, keeping to the road itself now that concealment was not his aim.

After a stop to nibble some cold snake meat and dried plums he had brought along, his concentrated forward progress, now with the fork of the crutch padded with an empty pouch stuffed with Spanish moss, was interrupted mid-morning as the rattle of wagon wheels behind him drew closer. Side-stepping into the brush at the roadside, he turned and saw a rattling old wagon pulled by a mule and an old paint mare, the driver pulling the odd team to a halt near where Two Hawks stood. A thick wave of scent then washed over him, hides of deer and otter and at least one bear mixed with the smell of a white man who had not bothered to bathe in a very long time.

"Hey, you, Caddo, there," the old trapper said, and loosed a thick stream of tobacco juice toward Two Hawks' left moccasin, the Indian looking up without moving his foot, a splash of the brown fluid gouting his moccasin's side. "Why didn't you move your durn foot? You saw it coming."

Showing neither anger nor amusement, Two Hawks looked up at the full-bearded man, his chin hair a mat of dried spit. "Well, old Caddo, what you doing out here, middle of nowhere, all tore up or at least broke in the leg? Some old squaw woman get tired of feeding your old bones and run you off?"

"This is not nowhere to me," Two Hawks said, and shifted his loads a bit to ease the pressure on his crutch. The tension hung in the air like a pall of smoke.

"You got money or something of value, I will give you a spot on the wagon here, take you on down the road …" But Two Hawks just slowly shook his head. He knew that more than one Indian and white man had vanished along this road in Neutral Ground for less than a few coins.

"Well, come on, Indian, climb on up and let's parle-vous or whatever it is you can talk." And the trapper winked. "I been around so much country we can find some kind of lingo—aw, hell." He wrapped the reins around the handbrake and stepped onto the wheel. "Lemme give you a hand, if you won't bite me. You ain't the friendliest Caddo I ever met—Come on, you want to ride or stumble on down this road all day?"

This old man had no shortage of words once he got started, Two Hawks thought, but understood that the other man's earlier belligerence had only been a series of tests, as much for the trapper's peace of mind as anything else. You didn't get old here by being stupid or naïve.

"Name's Jake O'Donnell, Jake Trap they call me. You?"

The Caddo considered before answering, but had heard of this fellow, not bad things. "Two Hawks I am called."

"That don't surprise me, the way you look, and that musket you are toting—heard Samuel did that work for you, back in Natchitoches. You been around parts about as long as I have, off and on—wondered when I might run into you."

"I have heard of you, Jake Trap. You have been a friend to the Caddo, and no coyote."

"I would sometimes like to be tricky as one of them coyotes, on four legs or two, but I ain't that smart."

Two Hawks wrinkled his eyes in amusement, after settling himself in the wagon, knowing well that a lack of intelligence was not this old man's problem. "But tell me, Jake Trap, why the horse and the mule? Are not the skins bringing enough money for a team?"

"I had two mules and a horse, too, old son, down south of here a while back, getting some Lipan to help me gather some buffalo hides to bring up to these parts." He saw the Caddo's attention pique at the mention of the tribe's name. "Them Lipan can be real mean, but good for me they hate Mexicans more than me, so they played along, but still and all they are brothers to the other Apaches further west, and, well, patience was wearing thin all around. Now, I been further west and know something about them Apaches, so I figured I would put on a little feast, a celebration of our hunt together before I headed out, and maybe so's I *could* head out ... I knew their brothers out west had them a favorite meat, so—"

"You ate one of your mules?" Two Hawks also had known of the Apache's penchant for mule.

"It was him or me, I figured. But what a roast! We ate most of one day and into the night, a few of those Lipan using some herbs so's they could purge and then eat more. I will tell you, them Apaches ain't wrong—that's some fine meat. Though a waste of a wagon team."

"But ..." Two Hawks hesitated, already knowing that Jake needed little encouragement to continue.

"Well, I think you understand this, being a gentleman of considerable years like myself, that when we get more 'mature,' I might say, we do not need quite as much freight, if you get my drift. I hitched up my saddle horse alongside the remaining mule early the next morning and beat a quiet retreat back east. Oh, they knew, and they let me go, maybe because they were so full of mule they couldn't be bothered to get up. And to tell you the truth, that paint mare was more than a little confused in the traces for several days, but before too long, she got the hang of it. Pulls good, most days, though sometimes she swings that big hammerhead around and rolls her eyes at me, as if to say, 'You know what in Hell you doing, Old Man?' I cannot give her a sure answer about that, I'll tell you, what I haven't missed having a saddle horse, nor feeding three sets of shoes."

And thus the day wore on, after a time Jake Trap talking over his shoulder once Two Hawks made it understood that the rattle of the unsprung wagon seat was causing him considerable pain. Upon Trap's suggestion, the Caddo gingerly shifted his cramped body to the piles of odiferous but padded skins in the wagon bed, at least shifting and burrowing until a solid but resilient bed had been constructed.

Though Jake continued to converse throughout the day, fortunately Two Hawks had no real need to engage or respond. An occasional grunt was all the trapper required, and Two Hawks was able to nap frequently to replenish his energy.

Making camp that night, the two men busied themselves gathering wood and picketing the animals in the lush grass near a creek. Jake brought out an iron spit to roast the turkey he had impressively shot in the head from the moving wagon earlier in the day, Two Hawks taking on the chore of gutting and plucking the bird from the wagon bed as they rolled.

Before trussing up the turkey on the spit, Two Hawks pushed some wild onion and mushroom into the cavity, then rubbing the outside skin with more wild onion greenery and a sprinkling of coarse salt from his pouch.

"I got me a danged cook!" Trap exclaimed.

"I sometimes salt my meat with a bit of piss, sometimes theirs sometimes my own," he added after they had gnawed their way through the entire bird. "But maybe I should bring along some salt, as you do—mighty good." Two Hawks had noticed, though, that Trap had waited for the Caddo to take the first bites, reassuring himself the Indian was not poisoning him. Understanding, the guest had made a point of pulling pieces from several spots on the bird to show that none had been tainted. Certainly not offended, he found more reason to trust the other's scrupulosity rearing beneath an exterior of apparent haphazardness. Jake Trap was no fool.

Chapter 19

At the trapper's suggestion, they both bedded down in the wagon that night and thenceforward; as he pointed out, "Folks expect you to lay out your blankets on the ground, so they look for you there first. Sometimes that gives me a few minutes to judge a man's reason for coming to my camp after sundown. Besides, I might get a snake or other creature now and again, but them big old heavy snakes with the poison tend to be lazy old things and won't bother themselves to lift their heads and try to drag them old coils up this high. Unless there's floods," he added.

Two Hawks thought the man had finished, but Jake continued. "Then you'd better look out. Been times I've whipped a team across a swollen creek or over-run bottom land, the mud sucking at the hooves and wagon wheels and them cottonmouths, seemed like they were just crawling all over that murky water, me slapping the team's backs with the reins in one hand, damned old Mandan coup stick in the other, throwing snakes, crushing their heads, seemed like times I was driving a wagon of worms—yeah, Mandan, way up north in the long-grass country, up past the Osage—" and Trap sat up, reached under the front seat to pull out a long notched stick with a curved end, the length bound with sections of leather strap, some beaded. "Eagle feathers come off a few seasons back. No ceremony to the thing now, though the old boy who give it to me said how that stick had touched more'n a dozen braves. Old like us, he give it to me to lighten his load, wouldn't be counting any more coup."

And Two Hawks then told him of his own spirit journey far to the north back when he had still been a relatively young man, learning over those long seasons of the bitter, bitter cold and snow and ice the tribes to the north withstood, but the clever ways, too, they adapted, digging trenches lined with stones so the large outside fires would transmit their warmth inside the wigwams during the coldest nights, and of the fresh water sea that appeared to have no end. At last, he brought out his fire pouch, unwrapped his striking steel and passed it over to Trap.

Jake turned it over in his fingers, sliding his four fingers beneath the striking face, admiring the coiled horns of the ends as they filled his hand when he bent his fingers to make a striking motion. "Beautiful, Caddo. I never saw nothing like it—got this at a fur-trading outfit of the Northwest Trading Company, you say? English—yes, I can believe that. No, my steel is nothing like this, old piece of trade steel—see? You get these anywhere."

Two Hawks took the old man's fire-starting steel in his old hands, noted its solid practical heft. "We trade?"

"Trade? That would be a steal," Jake said, chuckled at his own pun "Stea—steel—hear it? But that would do you wrong, to take this very special object of your memory ..."

"You would do me wrong not to accept the trade, Jake Trap. I have enjoyed its beauty for many years, true, but my admiration has grown stale. Enjoy its beauty—" He pushed the man's hand with the English steel back toward him—"freshly."

"Well, then, old son, I will, and I thank you for it."

The next day, with Two Hawks helping, Jake was able to break camp and hitch up the mismatched team within a short time, though while Jake lingered with adjusting the traces and attaching the double-tree, he felt an urgency in the Caddo's movements but knew enough not to press for an explanation. In time, the other man would explain.

Both men knew a great deal about solitude, not loneliness but the security of a comfortable alone-ness, and thus understood each other as few could. When someone spends days, months, years alone in the forest, in the swamps or on the plains, a person learns what lies inside as well as out, and you either lose your mind or find it—there is little in between. There is plenty of time for the enormity of the world to make itself felt, and a person will learn what to do with that—where you fit, and, yes, why you should put one foot in front of another.

Some don't. Two Hawks and Trap had both come across a few of the latter, old men or ambitious-looking young ones, some having obviously lived alone, a few with a fresh-dug grave not far from the cabin or even tent, the ones who think ahead or care to hang themselves from a tall limb. You at least usually had time to dry out a bit with just the crows getting the soft parts. If you were hasty or a bit short on nerve and didn't think you could withstand the preparation necessary for a rope, you used your musket, the longer models requiring a big toe through the trigger guard, though even with a gun things could happen: the powder could be too damp to ignite, or worse, as Jake knew. He had found a settler once up on the Colorado outside a dugout shelter hastily cut back into the riverbank, a young man in wool trousers and a dirty linen shirt, presumably the fresh grave that of his wife at the base of a clay outcropping nearby.

Though the man's horses had spooked and run off sometime earlier, or maybe he had just cut them loose, the saddle and side-saddle already had a bit of loose sand up their sides, and the couple's packs had already begun to be pried open by raccoons and such, but the gear still had the look of promise—the frontier would be kind to them, they had thought, the new country would open itself to them like a flower, and they would gather the bounty of new ground and love each other and raise a family in God's sight.

Or so they must have imagined. Perhaps it was a sudden illness or a fall from one of the horses—no matter. And just as suddenly, the man had found himself alone, with the corpse of his lovely wife. With no shovel in their gear, the new widower had industriously gathered some hand-sized clam shells from the exposed portions of the riverbed and dug out a deep grave in the scree of the bluffs—the broken shells and his ravaged fingers quickly told that story.

His body took a bit more thought, though the final event had probably occurred only a few days earlier.

The man's right boot was off, his bare toe bruised from the trigger guard of his musket but the bruise at least a day or two old and healing. Though the crows and buzzards had begun their work, the fatal gunshot was still recognizable, and the final trigger pull had been hasty, probably with eyes closed, the muzzle not socketed into his mouth but obviously held near his face. The ball had angled upward along the cheek, caromed off the eye socket and exited near the left temple—more importantly, the shot had not been immediately fatal, passing through the front portion of the brain. He had taken days to die.

Well, Jake explained to Two Hawks, he did not pack a shovel, either, "So I recovered what I could from their kit and left him where he lay."

Two Hawks' mind was already back on that earlier "suicide" he had unraveled in a very different way, the Hasinai ear spool situation, and how he, and others, were living with the aftermath. His solitude, he sensed, was very different from that of Jake Trap, who was obviously comfortable with living alone for extended periods of time but relished human interaction, too. Jake was loquacious and honestly reflective in public, giving of self yet patient with the peccadillos of those with whom he was conversing. Two Hawks, he admitted to himself, did not care for the company of others but was not against it—neither social nor antisocial, more ambivalent or asocial, he then surprised himself as he began to explain to Jake Trap the past circumstances that had led up to his present pursuit, coming to the conclusion, to himself of course, that he simply needed help.

Later, the wagon rolled onto a more packed clay street of what may one day become a town, Jake nodding politely to a couple of run-down-looking farmers loading seed into the back of a warped buckboard, touching the brim of his slouch hat to an older woman in a gingham dress and bonnet. She pressed her lips together and turned her head away.

Two Hawks kept his head lowered, feigning sleep, not looking directly at anyone, knowing that such curious glances would be read as insolence by some.

At the western edge of the settlement, Trap pulled the team over beside the Taylor Mercantile and Post, an exaggeration by the looks of it, wrapping the reins around the handbrake. (Two Hawks had come to see this as a formality, since those two equines were obviously not rushing off anywhere). "You coming in, old sir?"

Two Hawks lifted his eyes just enough to look at Jake. "Me stupid Indian—just stay in wagon," he said, and creased his eyes and mouth in a twinkling grin. "Maybe buy old Indian some sugar for tea—I have coins."

Some twenty or thirty minutes later, Jake came back through the open doorway, laughing back over his shoulder at something someone had said in farewell, but then his expression turned to puzzlement, even concern, as he hoisted himself back up the wheel and settled onto the driver's bench.

He reached into his vest pocket and tossed a dark brown cone as long as a man's hand but tapering to only a finger or so thick to the waiting Caddo, who turned it over in his hand, scratched it with a nail and smelled the cane.

"Closer we get to Spanish parts, the more we see that cane sugar—they say it is easier to transport and keeps better ..."

But Two Hawks looked over at the trapper, searching out his eyes as Jake gathered the reins and clicked and slapped the team back into motion.

"Did you learn anything about the group of wagons? How far ahead ..." Two Hawks' voice trailed off.

"Well, I did, but something I heard I don't understand. The group of wagons, six of them, are a little more than a day ahead, got slowed down when a axle on one of the wagons broke fording a creek and they lost half a day fashioning a make-do to get them to San Augustine—"

"And?"

"And of course I asked without wanting to show too much interest—don't want to sound like trackers or renegades or nothing—about a woman travelling alone on her wagon with her older son, and the old man who run the store said he saw a woman and a young man who could be her son, but they were with a young Caddo brave, bare legs but a French shirt, all three of them carrying on a lively conversation as they passed—"

"Lively ..." Two Hawks' brow creased in consternation.

"He said they looked real friendly-like. You tell me the whole story? If you did, that's some wicked bad young son there, working his way in close, somehow."

Two Hawks worked over the possibilities in his mind. Young Snake may have met Margaret and her son and had a change of heart. Perhaps he was recognizing the futility, even the self-destruction, that lay in a revenge that ensnares innocent lives. But, no, the older man was not such a poor judge of character. The eyes of that boy had led straight to a pit, and Two Hawks had glimpsed the poisonous wriggling forms half-concealed in the darkness. She-de-ah had aptly named the child and then set about painting every scale, setting the fangs and aiming his life like a crooked arrow that may dip and swerve but then would inexorably seek what it had been fashioned to strike.

Chapter 20

Before first light of the preceding day, the damp and quiet darkness that pressed down on the DeWitt wagon group had been suddenly broken by the unmistakable snap of a musket hammer pulled back to full cock.

"You touch that pot, Indian, and I will put you in the ground." Peter was scared, never having actually aimed his rifle at a man with the possibility of killing him. He was proud of himself, though, at how he had worded his warning.

"I mean no harm, Peter," the young Caddo said and withdrew his hand from the stewpot lid before turning and smiling broadly at the young Hays.

Peter looked at the other man with suspicion. "How did you know—"

"I know all about you, and your mother, Madame Dupre."

"Why do you know? What do you want here? I stayed awake to see who was stealing our food—"

"Try to forgive me. I grew hungry in the woods, following along until the right time."

"Time for what? To kill us? To steal our mules?"

"To bring you news of your old family friend, Two Hawks, my father."

"Two Hawks? He has no son, no children. He told us how his wife and children died long ago ..." Peter looked unsure, though he could not imagine that his old friend would have dissembled about such a thing as another child. Still, we all kept secrets.

"Well, you are correct, they did. But then he met my mother, one of those winter accidents, she told me, Two Hawks welcomed into my mother's dwelling, her husband having died some months before...I could not blame them—could you? And then he went on his way, not finding out about me for some years, and by then I was who I was and my mother ... no longer wished for another companion."

"But he knows you live?"

"Two Hawks knows about me, knows he created me ..." And the Caddo Snake looked into Peter's eyes in a way that made Peter feel like a rabbit had run over his grave, as his mother always said, though he couldn't say why.

"We will sit, then," Peter said, motioning with his musket, "and wait for Mother to wake up. We'll see what she has to say about your story—"

"No need to wait, son," Mrs. Dupre's voice made both the others jump, coming from the darkness beyond the fire's dull glow, and she stepped from behind the bole of a large white oak into the growing dawn. "I heard everything. You think me a heavy sleeper, Peter, but forget that a mother is very sensitive to any unusual sounds or even feelings near her children, no matter how old those children may be."

"Madame Dupre, please forgive my intrusion, but I hoped Two Hawks would be with you—perhaps something detained him. I know he wanted to be here."

"You may ride with us on our wagon for a time, if you wish, and tell us what you know about Two Hawks, since clearly you know some things we do not." She decided to weigh his remarks for value. "What are you called?"

"Drake," he said. "I am called Black Drake, the one that resembles a young male mallard but never grows a green head. I was often mistaken for someone else," he said, and laughed.

And as the day went by, the three swapped stories of Two Hawks, Snake calling himself Black Drake always careful to portray his relationship or opinion of the elder Caddo as positive, sensing Margaret Dupre's eyes watching him, waiting to seize upon a false or condemning impression of her old friend.

But gradually, into the afternoon, both Margaret and Peter grew to enjoy the young man's humorous stories and easy laughter, coming, even, to entertain the idea that perhaps this wayward son of Two Hawks manifested the more positive and light-hearted qualities his father possessed but was unable to express.

It was this frame of mind that the three had illustrated to the trader as they had passed through Taylor's Store.

As Jake and Two Hawks topped a long hill, the newly constructed Fort Jesup lay before them like a crown of bright boards, the community alive with industry and movement: smoke rose from several open fires as well as from the large stone chimneys of the central fort building and what they soon learned was a large kitchen.

They saw several soldiers, their navy blue trousers and lighter blue wool tunics impressive in the morning sunlight, rows of brass buttons glinting even at this distance as the men turned or straightened. Only one man wore his shako hat, the others obviously at ease, though the general impression remained one of discipline and control.

"Well, old pard," Trap said, "civilization and government has come to our little corner of the wilderness. They will squeeze folks like us right out of these parts—it has been a while since I have trekked this country over here—any of your kind, Caddo, over here? I know the pox took a good many of your Yatasi and Natchitoches tribes over north and south of Natchitoches—"

"Most of the Caddo have been 'taken,' as they say, by the smallpox disease—if that is small pox, I asked Dr. John Sibley some years back, what is big pox? He told me there is a 'great pox,' they call it, but from what he told me of it, I am fortunate not to have encountered it. But there are not many of my people here any longer—there are some Choctaw and Coushatta from the east those Choctaw—"

"I hear you, friend. No one seems to get along with them hides."

"Between the Choctaws and the Osages to the north, we Caddo are set upon from all sides. Now the Americans want to buy all our land in Louisiana Territory—how can you *buy* land? I think you just buy the power to make others go away ..." Two Hawks had a swift vision of the last Caddo village he had visited, before the people were "moved on."

Chapter 21

Two Hawks recalled vividly one early morning when two small children had timidly snuck over to watch him start a morning fire, long ago when the Natchitoches Confederacy of the Caddo had been numerous, when he had lived each day with a rhythm of belonging:

"Aren't you up early, little tat'iti?
Come sit while I start my fire for tea.
What do I do? I wrap my hand in doeskin,
Holding my steel so—this foreign flint has
Cut my fingers too many times, but this kindling wool and
Flint is not the moss your mother arranges, and you note my steel,
The ends curled? Long seasons past I was given this tool
By an old man from another people far north of here ... But
This is a story for another day. Yes, the dried tree moss they
Use works well, but from where did it come? Ah, the sparks
I struck have brought life to my little kindle here. Hand me
Those small sticks behind you ... The moss that hangs all
About us here—when first our people came to this place,
There and water, swamp, everywhere as it is now, but the
Trees growing out of the mud were bare, and our people of
The Caddo grew and planted our corn and squash and peppers,
Wove and bundled our lodges as we do today, and took deer
And bear as we pleased.

One day a man and his son came in a dugout shaped as we had
Never seen—Caloosa, they said, on a journey of the spirit, and
Showed us beautiful shells and a stick-thrown spear that was
Fast and true—they were a wondrous pair—and as they spoke,
The son, called Osceokla, looked deeply into the spirit of Dark

Moon, a tinuti maiden just blooded, her black shining hair falling
On either side, through her deep black eyes, his spirit reached,
And sat by her fire until they could not be apart. No, sihnuti,
He was not a skin-walker, as your mother warns you of, but
Only a youth feeling the love of a woman for the first time, as
She, lost in each other's hearts ... You will not understand for
A long time, but listen—Locksawee, the elder Caloosa, saw
His son slipping from his grasp, and Dark Moon's father saw,
Too, the two Caloosa with their journey not complete; Tichtow
Forbade his daughter to sit in the lodge when Osceokla sat with
His father; Locksawee, saw, too, the journey might end here,
Before the destined time, the two elders agreeing. And the two
Caloosa poled away on the morning of the next day, soon lost
In the mist that hung like the smoke of a memory over the track
Between the cypress trees, the hard light of day soon burning
Away any trace of where the men had gone, in all but the eyes
Of Dark Moon, whose thick lashes were stroked together into
Points by the slow tears of grief, not with sound of wailing or
Sigh but with the slow squeeze of deepening loss.
And day spun into day and into night, Dark Moon's bowl of corn
Meal and bright peppers untouched, joints of venison or even soft
Catfish unbroken in her lap, her long blue-black hair hanging
down
Her cheeks unbraided and unbrushed.

Until one summer day, Dark Moon, her strength failing, her heart
Knowing Osceokla would never return, wound her way through
Thicket and brush, past blackberry and clutching thorn, deeper
into
The swamp, wading through sloughs and past chuckling creeks,
Deeper into the cypress stands than ever she had known her
people
To tread before. And there she saw a cypress tree taller than all
The others, on a mound of mossed soil, the knees of the old tree
Rising up all around like the thick fingers of the yearning dead.
She propped a fallen trunk onto the bole and pulled herself onto
The lowest branch and began to reach up and climb, step and pull,

Until the surrounding trees fell away and the clean untouched breeze
Swept her face and lifted her tangled hair.

And there she took three long sinews from her brightly beaded
Pouch adorned with a glossy pink bit of shell Osceokla had given
Her. Twisting the sinews together she tied the cord around the one
Thick branch remaining, the other around her smooth throat, and
Spreading wide her empty fingers stepped off into the keening air.
And all that season Dark Moon's body swayed in the moving wind
And slowly dried, untouched by bird or furry hand, her black
doeskin
Shift hardened in the broken sun, her long blue-black hair caught
And lifted, turned as the season passed, lost its gloss and grew
from
Blue to dull black and then to moldy grey, the wind lifting her
Heavy tresses, until a long storm swept in out of the south, turning
Slowly as the water turns in my tea here. And the powerful winds
Pulled at Dark Moon's corn-husk form from side to side until her
Hair was drawn from the leathered skull, was pulled and caught,
Caught and drawn from tree to tree, from where the sun comes up
To where it goes down—her hair grey and swollen with grief drapes
Still from our branches. Such moss cannot kindle my fire, though
Many use it to. Yes, children, that is why the moss in the trees
Sometimes makes you sad.

Here, now, that happened long ago. Taste these berries I dried
Into sweetened spots for my tea."

His vision dissolved into daylight, and his smile was swept
downstream by the trapper's voice: "Which is why the Choctaws and
Coushattas and Alabamas are here, ain't it, Two Hawks, because settlers
got all their land back east. But, old son, I have no land and don't want any
that can be bought—which is why I am going west to the far
mountains—more land than anyone could ever buy or own, least in the
years I have left in these old bones—damme, I never met a dog I liked,"
Trap said, as the first dogs of Fort Jesup began barking outside a cabin's

86

door near the settlement's outer bounds. "Lest it was on a spit."

The two men were rattling into the fort's perimeter over some of the gravel cast on the road to control the spring mud.

"Hey, Caddo, you ever et dog—young ones, I mean."

"In a stew I have, on the edge of the great grasslands north of here—tender enough as pups," Two Hawks said, "but they get strong, almost like wild cats—when a thing eats another animal as its only food, it gets that strong taste. Bear is strong, too, but the berries and fruit they eat seem to calm it down a bit—but for the smell."

"I ask a simple question," Trap mumbled, "and get a damned connoisseur ..."

A young soldier not more than twenty years old stood at the side of the road, his tunic unbuttoned, boots muddy. He returned Trap's nod with a suspicious look, a stare of challenge at Two Hawks.

"Damn greeners," Trap said to Two Hawks. "Ever eat a man?"

"No, but I have been eaten—"

"Old man, you are going to drive me clean out of my brain ..."

But then Two Hawks briefly related his encounter with the Karankawa, as the wagon rolled past a deep excavation in the bright red soil, three bark-stripped logs each an arm's length thick waiting their turn behind the current log that two men had pinioned, one with a foot on it while the other steadied it, both gripping the long handles of a ten-foot saw drawn back and forth with the aid of two other men beneath the log in the pit, a stack of rough thick boards inches thick lay drying nearby—the forenoon air redolent with yellow pine and resin.

"I would rather wrestle a gut-shot mountain lion than do that kind of work, pard."

"When the boards come, Jake Trap, we stand on bought land."

"Careful, Indian—you might be turning into a poet. I heard a man reading some once back over near Baton Rouge a few year back, lot of the words sounding the same—almost like the bible but new ..."

"Words win wars—"

"There you go again, Caddo—"

"And end lives," Two Hawks added, thinking about Snake and what he might be planning, what he might have already done. They passed a half-circle of what were obviously barracks and storage buildings, before pulling to a stop near a set of wide steps leading to the second floor of the dominant building, a stone fireplace and chimney anchoring its western end.

"Must be the headquarters," Jake said, and secured the reins. The fort had only been constructed two years earlier. Two Hawks sat back on a stack of deer hides behind the wagon seat, making no move to climb down, but stretched his splinted leg out and propped it at a higher level on the wagon's edge. The leg appeared to be mending quickly, though when he stood there was still a dull throb as the blood ran to his calf.

"Indian will wait in wagon," he said. "I want answers but no questions. Please, Jake," he added, knowing the trappers' propensity for conversation. "We must try to catch up with them—tomorrow."

Chapter 22

After Trap made his way softly up the steps in his moccasins, a young soldier, his musket cradled in his right arm, ambled over, accompanied by another young man about his own age but dressed in wool shirt and trousers, obviously a member of one of the settler families. One of the agreed-upon conditions from the Neutral Ground treaty was that neither the Spanish nor the Americans were to admit settlers into the area, though that condition was more honored in the breech. The Spanish forces were far away, and both sides knew the Spanish had little interest in enforcing their claim. Fort Jessup was simply another indication of the growing dominance of U.S. power.

"Hey, Indian," the civilian said, his tone clearly belligerent, "we don't sell no whiskey here." Both young men smirked and nudged each other. "My friend here says they have come to get you Indians out of here—stealing our horses and such—can't talk, old—"

"He talks with a knife," Jake Trap said. He had slipped up behind the boys and was now pressing his own knife tip to the base of the younger man's throat. The young soldier leapt back and began to level his musket.

"Boy, I will puncture your friend and throw this here knife into your belly before you get to full cock. Besides, you ain't even got a cap on the nipple."

The soldier glanced down, embarrassed, and then looked up to where Lieutenant Colonel James Many stood at the top of the steps.

"Private McBain, go help Corporal Blake enlarge the latrine—and you go help them, William, or I'll have your Pa teach you some manners. Either one of these men, I expect, could remove your tongue and hand it to you between saying good and morning."

After the two young men attempted swaggers in walking away, Lt Col. Many turned to the older men.

"Jake Trap, and Two Hawks, he says your name is, obviously Caddo, come around to the back—I've a table set under an old cedar back there. Share some food with me, so's we can talk. Two Hawks, I heard of you a while back, something that took place up on Mule Bayou in Natchitoches—they call it 'Bayou Amulet,' sounds more pleasant and Frenchified than the old waterway named after the Spanish mules used to graze around and color the water—appears that you had a spill there, Mr. Two Hawks—it broke, is it?"

Jake was helping Two Hawks step gingerly down onto the wagon hub and then to the ground before the Caddo tucked his crutch into his armpit and hobbled toward the side of the building.

"I met a man who did not agree with me," Two Hawks began.

He had decided to share his story with the fort's commander. Not knowing what the coming days would bring, he preferred to share his perspective of the situation with authorities in this case, especially since the outcome might involve or entangle Margaret Dupre and Peter Hays. Usually an extremely private man who preferred to take care of his business and melt back into the woods, he did not wish untidy or questionable situations to follow his friends into the new colony.

"Colonel," Two Hawks began, easing onto one of the short stools around the rough table and making sure the two whites had seated themselves, "perhaps you had heard about a Caddo woman stabbed years ago inside a storehouse in Natchitoches." He saw the commander's eyes look down uncomfortably.

The colonel mumbled, "I had heard maybe you were 'involved' in that ..."

A servant brought out a pewter tray holding several pieces of cornbread and some smoked sausages. She returned a moment later with pewter mugs and quickly left, her head down.

As the men began eating, Two Hawks tasted the liquid in his cup and looked up in mild surprise, raising his brow in a question.

"I know what's good when I find it, Caddo," the colonel said. "That sassafras tea your people make—I prefer a bit more sugar than they do, but I'm growing to where I prefer it to the English tea."

The other two men chewing, Two Hawks sipped his tea and unfurled his tale, from She-de-ah's murder of her husband to the present predicament that he was seeking to remedy.

"Well, that just does not sound like Black Drake, the young Caddo I met travelling with the Dupre woman and her son—that was a bright and cheerful and cordial young man, flashing his smile and helping Madame Dupre down from the wagon with a shy humility. I just cannot reconcile that with what is clearly a despicable character. I consider myself a reasonable judge of human character—"

"Colonel," Two Hawks interjected quietly, "Black Drake is Snake. I have known bad people of every color, but I have not yet encountered a being who could sheathe and unsheathe his viciousness as soundlessly, without you ever guessing he was armed."

"Two Hawks," Col. Many said, "I have not lived as many years as either one of you two, and I may not have the wisdom and experience, but understand my position here and the position of Cantonment Jesup. The times are rapidly changing, as I am sure you are aware as well as anyone, perhaps even more so—I understand the tenuous position of the Caddo in this part of the country—"

"We are 'tenuous,' as you say, everywhere, Colonel."

"Yes, well, I am sorry for that, but this territory is not insecure, increasingly the opposite. My orders, my charge, is very clear, and the voice behind them resonates all the way to the President of the United States. While the original terms of the Neutral Ground treaty were agreed to by the Spanish and the U.S. governments, Spain has had little or no influence east of the Sabine River, other than to encourage our slaves to run away and give them safe haven on the Spanish land grants. And while President Jefferson said unofficially that the Louisiana Purchase to his understanding included all lands north of the Rio Grande River, I do not see that as accepted or understood by all parties just yet. However, my charge is to bring and/or enforce order in the Neutral Ground, for as long as that territorial definition remains the law of the land, and I do expect all of this territory at least to the Sabine and north to the big bend of the Red River, to very soon be an important part of the United States. With that said, and Xinasi Two Hawks, I am not saying anything you don't know already or at least have gathered ..." He paused.

Two Hawks nodded gravely, and put his right hand to his heart, his eyes glistening at the young man's knowledge of the Caddo terms of hierarchy.

"But, Caddo, I am a young man, not yet with wife or children, new to my journey. My world will be made on the frontier but lived out among my kind. I consider my charge here very seriously, and I see it as an important step toward what I trust is, in my hands, a successful future both for myself and for the United States. So please understand that while I consider your mission to be of great importance to you—"

"And of great importance to two people I care very much about—"

"Yes, Two Hawks, I applaud your concern and, well, strength of will, but hear me: do not carry out what you consider to be 'private justice' in the Neutral Ground, or I must come after you. I must uphold the rule of law, even United States law or at least the basic principles of justice as the law defines them. What happens on the west side of the Sabine River is not under the purview of my command—"

"If it can wait that long," Two Hawks whispered.

"Make sure that it does, Two Hawks. Respect my position and the position of my government. The river is only two days' travel by wagon from here, and I did not sense any danger—"

"Nor did I, Colonel," Two Hawks said, indicating his splinted leg. "I hear your words. I see your position here and I am glad for the path you foresee for your coming years, if not for the Caddo. If it is possible to do safely, I will wait. But my safety is not my concern. The boy was well named, or perhaps named and then trained to live up to it—I will not kill a snake, poisonous or not, if it is no imminent danger, but I know this one will strike, and I will not give him the chance to do it."

"Well, gentlemen, I will not keep you any longer. From that moisture blowing up from the Gulf—can you feel it?—I believe that we will get a round of rain coming in from the south in the next day or so. A considerable amount of that, as you know, will end up in the Sabine River, and I do not think either of you, or I, too, want you to be caught on the east bank with the colony wagons on the other. Gaines is an able man, from what I hear—yes, Gaines bought the ferry operation about two years back, has a place over on what folks call the 'Texas side,' a careful man, but that river rises fast. He'll shut down the ferry at the first sign of flood ..."

"Then good day to you," Jake said as he rose and extended his hand. "And we appreciate the victuals and the visit."

Two Hawks leaned on his crutch and got his left leg under him, levering to a standing position. "I am in your debt, Colonel, and I do appreciate your knowledge of my people."

Chapter 23

Later that day, Jake Trap spit past the wagon's juddering wheel, saying, "Damme, Two Hawks, that colonel's still green but he gets right after it. I would not like to look back and see him on our trail. He give us fair enough warning—"

"That young colonel is no fool. I, too, would prefer not to stand between him and what he sees as his duty. Still, if he hears something of what might occur—"

"A well thought move, Caddo. We had best get on down the road a distance before nightfall—that ferry is a good day and some away. That leg coming along? Your turn to find us some supper—and no more snake."

"Do you have an iron pot, Jake Trap? Good—I woke early and found a visitor, wrestling with that turkey carcass I had tied to a fallen branch. A raccoon, stewed in some dried fruit and onion, and I see a sack of corn meal ..."

"You old hide, we stay together much longer and I'll be fat as a goose tied to a stake. Then you'd be makin' a pa-tee outen this old liver."

Two Hawks did not understand but asked for no explanation.

The forested hills grew longer and steeper as they rolled west, each crest now approached with caution as neither man wished to be surprised at what might lay revealed in the next trough, but the mid-morning revealed only one other traveler: a wagon driven by a local settler, his two children staring in open wonder at the old trapper and his Caddo companion. The young man was coming, he had said, from a growing settlement of Baldwin's Store and tavern, near San Jose Creek, a few miles ahead, making the trip to Natchitoches for fresh seed and a plow he had ordered from England.

With the wagons pulled to a halt abreast of each other on the narrow road, the travelers swapped a few stories and concluded by Trap's passing over a beaver pelt in exchange for a small slab of smoked bacon and two twists of tobacco.

After they had moved on, Two Hawks said casually, "I can see why you do not have money for another mule—you are chewing your wealth away—"

"Ye gods, man," Trap said, feigning irritation. "Beginning to sound like I have a wife scolding me for wasting my wealth. I don't want another team. These two old hayburners I am accustomed to now—kind of like me, and you, too, I might add—they just clump along, not with any particular speed or beauty, not really much to look at, but that makes them not much for someone else to want, if you get my meaning—safer that way."

"I understand, Jake Trap, and I am glad to have your assistance, though I did not truly understand the lack of worth in us both, and the value of worthlessness, until you explained it," Two Hawks said, smiling, but then turned more serious as he reviewed in his mind what lay ahead. He and Trap had decided to meet with the wagon group at the evening camp. To approach the group during the day on the road would be to suggest that at least one wagon, the Dupre's, slow down or stop, the other wagons probably following suit in consideration and defense.

Even without encouragement, Jake's odd team moved more quickly than the other wagons, at least three of them heavy with supplies and a few cherished pieces of furniture, iron bedsteads and one dresser from a Boston furniture maker carefully wrapped with new tarps. Nearly everyone wanted a new start and would construct new lives but needed perhaps one piece of home, a physical manifestation of family or loved ones left behind.

Trap's wagon rattled along through the heat of the day and into the lengthening shadows cast by the towering trees, keeping the tail wagon of the other group several hills ahead of them, barely out of sight. Jake and the Caddo did not want to alarm the group, as indeed they might become, thinking of a lone wagon trailing them without attempting contact.

While sometimes patrolled by soldiers from the new fort and understood to be a more trafficked road, the Camino Real still held dangers other than those of weather. Most runaway slaves from Louisiana plantations, often accompanied by Spanish deserters or in some cases Anglos wishing to foment rebellion, in most cases sought the less-traveled trails and crossings to avoid detection and exposure. But as more than one lone unwary rider or wagon had discovered to their misfortune, one could not expect the captives of legal indenture to honor the principles of moral and ethical conduct of the society from which they sought refuge. There were plenty of lawless men, and women, too, plying the road, some with reason for hatred, some simply bad or ruthless opportunists.

Late that afternoon, the wagon with Two Hawks and Jake approached another wagon pulled off into the low brush at the bottom of a long hill, and they were reminded of the aura of mystery and peril that the trail often imposed almost like the drape of a loose shroud.

As they drew closer, the men could see that the teamless wagon had stood in that spot for some time, canted at an angle, the bed twisting from two missing wheels. The wood had begun to weather and, as happens very quickly in the sunlight, the wild grapes had wound their way through, over and under the bed and seat, the wagon tongue already lost in broad leaves and tendrils.

The wagon stank of desolation. "Could be some local farmer just broke down and decided it was time to build a new wagon," Trap began.

"Still would have dragged this one back for parts," Two Hawks said. "Some good wood was left. Besides, that's a heavy wagon, made to move settlers, but perhaps they were part of a larger group and the occupants climbed aboard others' wagons and moved on."

"Mebbe," Jake said.

But both men left unspoken the more likely possibility, that the wagon's occupants had simply vanished. More often than most travelers chose to admit, the seemingly impenetrable walls of the forest and brush on either side of the old trail was periodically inhabited by ragtag bands or isolated miscreants of every stripe and origin, many of whom had no qualms or hesitation about killing the inhabitants of an entire wagon for a brass-buttoned vest and some bacon, or a morning desire to rape a red-haired girl.

Sometimes the victims were found, but as often as not, as with this derelict wagon Jake was passing, the folks were simply dragged some distance into the woods and abandoned, with only the circling birds or sickly-sweet stench of decay brought to those on the Camino by a strong breeze.

Folks often did not stop to investigate, saying to themselves or their companions, "old bear died back there, I figure," or "somebody's cow wandered off," in part because they did not want to find another human being in there, which would require some sort of Christian response of digging a grave or reporting the incident, taking part or even most of a work day.

In part, they did not investigate because they did not wish to acknowledge to their families or themselves "that there be monsters in those woods."

Chapter 24

Two Hawks told Jake about one wagon he had once encountered out west of the ancient Caddo mounds near where the old Camino Road trail turned south toward San Antonio and eventually Mexico City—there were other trails winding from there across the increasingly open country toward the far blue mountains where the old trading center of Santa Fe remained a vibrant town. As had been his habit for a very long time, Two Hawks had been on foot. For him, a horse was an announcement and a temptation; besides, he had not been in a hurry in many years, learning, too, years ago, that a determined hunter on foot could usually outlast most large game, on four feet or two, if he kept to the chase with enough tenacity.

He had seen the circling birds, their wing tips like black and bony outstretched fingers, an hour's walk before reaching the wagon. The canvas covering was still intact, so he had first thought the birds at work on livestock, but on approach he noted that the vultures were squabbling over forms that lay too low on the ground to be the ribcages of horses or mules or cattle. The wagon's inhabitants had been dragged into a low copse of blackjack oaks only a stone's throw from the trail, here a dried track through the beginnings of rolling grass-covered hills. The torn broom-straw track leading from the wagon clearly indicated that the victims had been very much alive at the time.

Two Hawks had seen bodies before, had witnessed killings in various stages of ferocity, had even himself killed when necessary, but, as he said and Trap agreed, these killings and mutilations were in some dark way different. Two Hawks guessed the settlers had been overtaken only the day before, the birds beginning on the soft tissues of the face but not yet having progressed to the abdominal swellings in the heat.

The male, his youth evident by a whispy reddish beard, had been gut-shot, beaten about the head, probably by musket butts, one defined indentation suggested, and had finally died of blood loss, his genitals, clearly removed while his heart still pumped, stuffed into his mouth.

The young woman's skirts had been entirely removed and she now lay clad only in the remnants of her blouse and chemise torn open, deep bite marks crusted with blood on her breasts. The blood smears between her legs told that she had been used numerous times over the course of the day, the stained rock near her head perhaps used to stun but not allow her to fall into the mercy of unconsciousness. Her infant was jumbled at the base of a small oak, the bark of which still smeared where the child's head had made contact.

"The tracks of shod horses and a few brown stains of tobacco juice told me these were white men," Two Hawks said solemnly to Trap.

"I do not doubt you, old son," Jake said. "But I expect that both you and me have found our share of red renegades, too."

"This I know," Two Hawks said. "I understand as well that at times we may kill each other very slowly to, well, probe the depth of our foe's courage or endurance. I understand that, though I haven't taken any pleasure in that sort of examination—"

"Apaches do that," said Trap. "As do Comanches."

"But these isolated killings and, well, 'murders,' you people call it—these are not braves, warriors, doing the killing—the victims are simply people, suffering and killed because someone enjoys it. Revenge I understand—believe me, I understand. But just to kill for pleasure, without more reason than this—the animals do not do this."

"Been told a weasel will get into a hen house and kill every chicken, gets into a thirst for blood and just keeps on killing—" said Trap.

"Perhaps. I have felt a bit of that, on the tribal battlefield, that exhilaration, to keep on ..." Two Hawks confessed. "But wolves do not, or panthers or even coyotes. Mostly just us—because a weasel will eat at least one, the hunger a rhythm in the earth. This desire in some of us, color does not matter, is like a hidden disease, like some people may suddenly get sick and die, in great pain, and we cannot find a cause, though Dr. Sibley told me once that many of these people have large masses of bad flesh in different parts of their bodies that just begin to grow—'cancers' he called them, I remember. Perhaps we should catch some of these murderer people and cut them open, look for cancers in their heads somewhere ..."

"I hope you plan to do the cutting once they are dead, you old Caddo," Trap said. "I know I can talk, like to chew the fat, matter of fact, and when I first met you back there on the Camino, I figured you to just be another old hide back there in the wagon, but once you mount up on a thing, you sure do ride it to exhaustion."

"Your civilized world has given me too much time to think."

"What does that mean?"

"Back when each village had to grow food and hunt for food," Two Hawks began.

"Lord, back to the Flood," Jake rolled his eyes.

"The Caddo have such a story, too," Two Hawks said.

"Never you mind that one. When you all 'had to grow food and hunt' ..." Jake encouraged.

"Make pots and utensils, make weapons and dwellings and cure hides, we stayed busy. There was very little time to simply think about general matters, great matters. Now that most of those things are made by someone else, so many people responsible for one thing, then each person with one thing less to make, we just need the money to buy them, and then bad things happen."

"You think your people were better off, happier, before the white man came?"

"Yes, but I do not blame the white men. It is simply change, and some of it is good and some bad. In many ways, thinking is a curse. We were happier, happy, really, because the Caddo are not *less* happy now—we are *not* happy—but we were happy when we had fewer *things* and much less time to *think*. Thinking leads to unhappiness ..."

"Well, then, old pard, let's stop doing it for a time and just chew." Jake pulled off a piece of his tobacco twist and looked off into the distance ahead of the wagon team. Two Hawks could see, though, that his fellow traveler had continued to muse. After a few moments, Jake's chewing stopped. He spit and shifted the chew into his cheek. "But from what you say, and what I heard about you finding out people's secrets, sounds like you think all the time. You must be the unhappiest person alive."

"Perhaps one."

As they made camp in the growing darkness near the top of a long hill, further from the water but with a clear line of sight in both directions, both men felt in their bones they were drawing closer to their quarry. Building a fire just east and below the crest of the hill, they moved about their tasks silently, Jake collecting firewood and stones, setting up an iron crossbar for the pot, and Two Hawks skinning and trimming the raccoon that had been gutted and cut to drain earlier in the day.

A distant gunshot froze both men in mid-motion, and they processed the sound for distance and direction.

"Ahead of us, less than a mile," Trap said, and Two Hawks nodded in agreement.

Now clear to the two men, the colonists were intending to reach Gaines Ferry the following day. This would be new territory to the following men. Going west and returning earlier, Trap had used Myrick's Ferry up at Brown's Bend, or Hamilton's Ferry, though both did not provide a direct route to Nacogdoches along the old Camino Real, now often called the San Antonio Road. However, he only afforded these ferries when he had a wagon.

On foot or on horseback, both he and Two Hawks had made frequent use of one of several shallow fords that could be waded, the one most often used being the Spanish ford, variously known as Salstre Prairie or the Pass of Salines or even the older Arroyo de las Boregas.

One of the real advantages of the Spanish ford was that it was an old Spanish trail that went through older Spanish land grant communities and was traveled by Spanish citizens who often made crossings into Louisiana without official permission.

But there were disadvantages for the same reasons. The ford was also frequently used by outlaws, runaway slaves, and Spanish deserters. One needed to keep his wits about him and a musket ready to hand.

Taking time breaking camp and harnessing the team in the morning, Two Hawks both understood the colonists' choice of Gaines. The approaching road had been recently reconstructed, back in 1819, and since the ferry was a busy crossing, American soldiers patrolled frequently. Renegades usually chose another route, which was also somewhat reassuring when Two Hawks thought about Snake implementing something in the open. Perhaps the young Caddo would wait for the other side of the river where authorities were scarce, at least outside of San Augustine.

Slowly topping the summit of the next long hill, so as not to encounter others before they were ready, Trap and Two Hawks were presented with a straight stretch of road running through the swampy forest, but no wagons or horses were to be seen.

The mysterious shot was solved when, less than a mile further on, Two Hawks indicated some trampled brush on the north side of the road. Jake handed him the reins and leapt nimbly down from his seat, easing forward into the tall grasses.

"Well," he said, holding up a bloody skin with the head of a white-tailed buck attached, "somebody's supper got too curious. No time or need for the hide, nor for us, neither. That was quick work. And from the depth of these wagon ruts, these folks must be our people, close enough to catch up to them at our choosing."

Chapter 25

The old Caddo and Jake Trap had joined the group of wagons just as the sun had shot its flames into the tattered clouds and slid below the beard of mixed hardwood trees that evening. Peter squatted and stared into the embers of the evening cookfire, lost in his thoughts, as Snake soundlessly stepped from behind a hickory trunk and approached from behind, his right arm upraised with something filling his hand.

"Lower your arm or die, Snake," Two Hawks said from behind him, in an intense whisper heard by Peter as well.

Snake turned, shock and surprise showing on his face. Peter, too, twisted on the balls of his feet, looking back over his shoulder, saying, "Two Hawks, what are you doing? Why have you drawn your knife?"

"Please, Xinesi," the younger Caddo said, the innocent look of surprise clear as water on his face. "I am not this 'Snake' you speak of—I told you. You are mistaken. I am Black Drake, and, accept it or not, I am your child."

"Open your hand," Two Hawks said, balancing on his left leg and crutch, his knife steady in his right hand.

"This?" Snake said. "An amulet, a silver amulet a priest gave me once—see?—to keep me safe. I want my new friend Peter to have it, to keep him from harm on this new journey," and he smiled brightly to the still-crouching Hays. Two Hawks was amazed, alarmed by the boy's talent for dissembling.

"What is wrong with you, Two Hawks?" Peter said. "You are not yourself. Ask Mother to look at your wound—you may have a fever or something. This man means me no harm—see that. Could he be your son?"

Two Hawks sheathed his knife awkwardly and gripped his crutch, looking closely from Peter to the other man who, out of Peter's view, slowly closed and opened his eyes, twisting his mouth into a smirk as he did so.

Peter accepted the talisman from the outstretched hand and smiled affectionately. "Thank you, my friend. I will wear it, confident in the knowledge that others care about me." He was trying to emulate the formal pronouncements he had heard older men make when they spoke at formal occasions. "And you, my old friend, please control what I needs must conclude are the misguided fears of an older man. I am grateful for your concern but am embarrassed ..."

But Two Hawks had already turned and was limping toward Trap's wagon. Snake had outsmarted him—the scene had been planned from the outset, the result that his adversary was held in even dearer regard by the boy, the latter now eying his old and trusted friend with suspicion, or at least doubt. The old Caddo shook his head in grudging admiration at the results, knowing that even if he shared the occurrence with Jake Trap, there was an even chance that the old trapper would begin to doubt Two Hawks' judgment, perhaps even his stability.

The faces around the morning fire were easy to read. Margaret and Jake were cordial, as were Peter and "Black Drake," but clearly the incident from the previous evening had been shared. Two Hawks several times caught what he concluded were veiled expressions of, well, study, if not quite caution, though the object of their concern was not as simple to

100

ascertain.

The wagons reached the eastern terminus of Gaines Ferry on the Sabine River shortly after midday, a Friday. Tied up on the other side, waiting for a load to carry across from the west so as to have paying cargoes in both directions, the ferry captain signaled that he would come across in one hour, and the wagon teams stamped in their traces as the teamsters and settlers readjusted and secured their loads, with a constant eye toward the south. Banks of dark grey-bellied clouds were piling up and blowing in from the Gulf on a steady south wind that began to gust more aggressively as they approached.

The first heavy drops, almost gouts of water, slapped the oilskin tarps like loose gravel. And then it came down.

Within minutes the travelers could not make out the other side of the river, the water beaten flat by the rain.

Impatient under his oilskin poncho, and hot, Peter said to both wagons waiting side by side in the downpour, "When will the ferry come across? I want to get to Texas."

"Will the ferry come is a better question, boy," Jake said. "They will not risk their livelihood because us folks are in a hurry. No doubt they will watch for a while."

"For what?" the young Caddo said.

Jake continued, "They will watch to see how fast the water rises and see how fast the color changes. Faster it gets red and brown, the faster the run-off, and that might include other things."

"What do you mean, 'other things'?" Peter asked, thinking the trapper was just another old worrier, afraid to risk much for a new adventure, something the young man had had too little of.

"We would not like to be out in mid-current," said Trap, "and see a full-grown pine tree shooting down on us with no time to get out of the way. Be a mess, that would."

And Peter thought about how quickly the bayous and even the Red River would swell to hands of water clawing at trees and even houses. The others, too, mentally thankful through visions of benign creeks and bayous in moments turned into treacherous floods. So they sat, lost in themselves, and waited.

But then, as quickly as it began, the rain ceased and the sun glared down, vegetation and the verdant earth steaming in the heat.

The sound of a brass bell rang over the water, and they looked up to make out the shapes of several men untying the lines from the flatboat ferry on the distant graded bank.

"Appears that Gaines would rather have some money in hand than gamble on another freight showing up going east," Jake said. "Water gets too high and fast and he ain't got nothing."

"I heard that ferry boat has space for two wagons," said John Carpentier, a young subsistence farmer with a wife and two small children but no slaves. He had sold everything and borrowed a bit from his older brother up in Tennessee. "Maybe they will give us a special rate for small wagons—"

"Hah!" Trap laughed. "I never knowed a ferryman to give no special rates. You best make sure you keep your children on the wagon or he might charge you an extra twelve and a half cents each for 'em."

"Ferriage is one dollar for a light wagon, two for a heavy one, what I heared," another teamster said. "Your old trapper's wagon the only one looks light to me. Unsaddle them horses and sit on a wagon," he said to a couple of outriders. "Loose horses twelve and a half cents, man and horse twenty-five."

"So just because they got a barge and a place on the river," Peter said, obviously irritated at the cost, "they just sit back and collect money from all the folks want to get to the other side—it does not look like a fair business to me."

"Some days it is, some it ain't," Trap said. "After you save up the money to buy the crossing and somehow get agreement from the gov'mint, two gov'mints in this case, to let you do it, then you wait. Some days, some weeks, it rains and rains and you can't do nothing. Then your cable breaks and you drift downstream and get some mules to help you pull the ferry back upstream to the spot where you keep the banks graded so's your loads can get on and off. Rest of the time you just wait and hope folks want to come—no sure thing. No law says they got to come use the ferry. I allow there's a good many days a dollar a wagon don't seem near enough."

"It sure is a bundle of money to us," Peter finally said, obviously rebuked for his short-sighted view of business but not wanting to admit it.

Chapter 26

Their exchange had been interrupted as the flat-planed bow of the ferry slid soundlessly into the wide berth scooped out of the riverbank at their feet, the water dredged deep enough there to receive the boat's draft when loaded. The thick hemp cable stretched up the graded bank to where it was secured to a stout water oak.

"Ladies, gentlemen, let us load with dispatch," the head ferryman formally announced. "We need to get you folks across before that water gets too fast. Wouldn't want half of you here and the other half waiting on the Spanish bank. I'll be collecting ferriage directly."

After payment was concluded and an assemblage of coins, including French and Spanish money, the American coinage not as common, were stowed in the ferryman's pouch, he looked over the wagons and livestock.

"All the same to you folks, load that heavier second wagon and mules with four loose horses—I want as much to balance the loads."

"Your boat, Mr. Oliphint," said William McIntosh, the unofficial wagon boss.

The ferryman led the mule team toward the graded ramp and the waiting flatboat, his mate slapping their rumps in encouragement, but even the mules were skittish, trying to plant their hooves but sliding forward reluctantly in the gravel and clay, eyes rolling. Oliphint looked at McIntosh, who just shrugged. "Can't say as I blame 'em much—them mules never been on no boat before, and mules like to be sure of things."

Shuddering, stamping impatiently, the mules finally pulled the heavy wagon onto the rough planking of the deck and were still, though both animals looked ready to jump over the side at the least provocation.

"Maybe we should trade places," the boatman suggested. "Let them see the man they know."

Four saddle horses were pulled on next, a good deal more vocal than their predecessors, but they seemed to be more willing, once they had seen that nothing frightening had happened to the mules. Their halter ropes were tied to the back of the wagon, their riders reassuring from the wagonbed.

"Cast off," the ferryman said, and his deckhand loosed the docklines and tossed them back up on the bank where they were tethered to heavy poles driven into the shore. Both men began to haul soundlessly at the cables, and the boat bit into the current and slid several feet downstream. The river and barge were quiet except for the creak of the thick rope where it ran through a cable eye on the rail and the nervous stamp of a mule's hoof. The passengers looked at each other with trepidation.

"You gentlemen lend a hand," the boatman said, "and we'll get over there a bit faster."

"You give us some of our money back for helping?" a man said nervously.

"Stay around a few days and help grade the bank and splice some new cable, I'll see about that," the boatman laughed, reminding the settlers that the actual crossing was only a small portion of the business.

With four men pulling at the cable, two holding the boat steady on landing, the trip across was accomplished in very little time, and the ferry was soon headed back for another load, though the men noticed that the level of the river's surface had risen almost a foot, a gradual murkiness threading the water.

Two hours later, though, the crossing was completed without incident, and relief showed on all the colonists' faces. The ferrymen snugged down the shorelines but with plenty of slack, having seen the water rise another two feet during that time, with no sign of slowing. Their business, they knew, would wait for the upstream runoff to abide.

The colonists had wanted to make San Augustine by nightfall, but the stress of the ferriage had exhausted several. Carpentier and his family, along with others, argued for an early camp set-up, and no one protested.

They had a number of well-trod clearings to choose from, as obviously folks going east or west had found themselves in a similar situation, though the well-used clearing always made collecting firewood a bit more taxing.

But even tired as he was, sixteen-year-old Peter Hays stole a long glance at Eudice Carpentier, John's wife, as she helped her small children down from the wagon to begin collecting wood for a fire. Not for the first time, Hayes noticed the sensual swing of her heavy braid of chestnut brown hair across her back, and as she raised her leg to help down their three-year-old daughter Patricia, she of necessity pulled up her full skirt and petticoat to give her leg more freedom of movement.

Peter's breath caught as he saw for only a moment the inside of her soft white leg just past the knee.

Eudice Carpentier glanced back over her shoulder, Patricia in her hands, and caught Peter looking. Embarrassed and blushing, he quickly looked over at the team still in harness. But did she turn back around with the faintest of smiles? Though not yet twenty-five, she must know what effects her full woman's figure had on a man. Did she really feel it necessary to raise her leg so high onto the wagon wheel's hub to catch her daughter under the arms, or was that for him? He was becoming increasingly tormented by his feelings toward Eudice, and by what those feelings caused to his body as he lay under his muslin mosquito drape each night.

These thoughts were not new to Peter, though he shamefully admitted that to him the arousal by another man's wife made him question his own strength of character. He knew this was simply wrong, Eudice was wrong to encourage what he could only call a dalliance—but then his memory of her inner thigh, leading to, well … he was lost in his blood's feelings and cared nothing about where such feelings might lead.

This seemed so much older, more mature, than the previous relationships and the consequent feelings he had shared, as well as he could, with other women, girls really, more his own age.

But none of them, or his friends back in Natchitoches really had any questions about, well, the mechanics of the thing. Surrounded by livestock, even in town, any child older than six had seen dogs, horses, cattle, coupling in order to reproduce, and it was difficult not to notice the fierce energy exerted by the male and the relatively passive acceptance of the female. Peter thought about the first time he had seen a pair of mallard ducks, or at least the first pairing. The boy had been very upset watching the male finally catch up with the female, seeing the mallard climb onto her back, pushing her completely under the water, pecking, grabbing, seizing the back of her soft-feathered head and driving it, too, under the water.

That duck is killing the other one, he had thought—he's drowning her, and he had shouted for the duck to "stop—stop hurting that duck," but the male was soon finished and swam away. Peter's friend Jack had laughed at him as the female doused herself a few times by digging her head under water and bringing the water over onto her back, after which she raised herself, flapped her wings a few times, tucked them down and swam away, unconcerned and obviously unharmed, though she was soon joined by another suitor.

"They're doing it," Jack had said. "Don't you know that's how they do it?"

Well, he did after that, though the cats were the most disturbing, still. He had not wondered or even noticed that, unlike dogs, cats had never shown themselves doing it. He had of course heard cats fighting—the warm spring nights were filled with the sounds of their vicious fighting, screeching at each other, growling, the rising tempo of their abandon, until they obviously pounced and tumbled in a screaming encounter, often punctuated, followed, by a long silence.

And he had seen the results of those midnight encounters, or at least the results of the fights. One tom in particular he would never forget—Peter named him Smoke, though the boy came to understand that the cat needed no name or anything else from human beings.

Smoke had belonged only to himself, and to the night. Obviously long abandoned or ignored by any human care or feeding, the tom was lean as a wild animal, long and low-slung, with short grey hair of a consistent length and deep smoke color over every inch of his frame. If I were to be an animal, this would be it: an inhabitant of civilization but not a part—supremely independent, supremely confident and physical, with no show or braggadocio, well, or at least not often, like that English poet he had read at the schoolteacher's house.

On some summer nights, the air hot and still, cicadas ringing in the trees, Peter would find refuge from his sweat-dampened sheets in going out onto the porch that faced Duchamp Street in Natchitoches, sitting in one of the wooden chairs under a wispy open-weave drape for the mosquitoes, and walking, well, pacing panther-like down the absolute middle of the street would come Smoke, yeowling low every thirty seconds, announcing his presence to any cat that cared to know.

One night Peter saw the cat angle over across the road to a four-foot lattice fence thickly wrapped with scuppernong grapes. Smoke stood momentarily and then calmly leapt up to the top brace that held the white fence, yeowled once, and disappeared on the other side as if the feat were just another step.

And after Smoke had one night walked calmly over to Peter's house, walked up the porch steps as though he owned them, walked over to the boy's chair, turned and shot two quick streams of urine on the chair leg in possession, Peter was furious, but just for a moment, before grinning and shaking his head in admiration. "You bastard," the boy had said aloud, and wished he had that kind of nerve.

Another night, determined to make Smoke his friend, Peter had smuggled out some scraps of stewed chicken skin to bribe the cat. Down the street Smoke came, and Peter hissed to get his attention, then dangled the pieces of skin to entice him over.

Oh, Smoke walked over—the boy had never seen the cat trot in haste, much less run—and calmly ate the chicken, after which he lay down on his side, head back, on the porch planks and closed his eyes.

Wanting the cat to play, Peter found a short twig, squatted down, and began to flick the cat's forepaws with it, first raising one and then tapping the pads of the other, growing a bit impatient, wanting to see the cat's claws.

The paw struck. Without rising, Smoke's front paw flashed out, caught the tip of Peter's thumb with a single claw, held it, and the cat raised his head calmly from the porch plank. He looked at the captured thumb, not even at Peter, found the prey uninteresting, released it, and put his head back down.

It was one of the most beautiful things the boy had ever seen. Admonished—admonished by an alley cat! "A paltry thing, this thumb," he imagined Smoke thinking, sending his message clear as carving it on a tree: "Don't play with me, boy! I don't play."

That was how he wished he could be with Eudice Carpentier, imagining that one day he would be down by the creek, cleaning a brace of geese he had shot on the wing, when down would stroll Eudice, bucket in hand, to get some water for supper. She would walk over the sand and stones, leaving her shoes on the bank, barefoot, lift her skirts to keep them dry, very close to where he sat on his hams, baring a breath-taking expanse of white calf and thigh, and, bending over to dip up a bucket of water, give him a sight of her full breasts filling the front of her shift.

She would straighten, still holding her skirts in her left hand, and he would rise as well, cast the geese up onto the rocks, and look into her hazel eyes. She would flush, the blush moving down to her long throat, and he would reach out, calmly, confidently, place his hand full on the side of her neck, and say nothing, but think, and she would know his thought, "I could have you, take you, here, or not." And like Smoke, with his thumb caught with one claw, transmit with his eyes, "I do not play."

And she would touch him.

But not today.

Chapter 27

The wagons passed through Red Mound, on the Texas side of the river, and all of the colonists were excited about arriving in this new territory, though they were also anxious and somewhat fearful, not of the terrain, as they noted heading west that the long hills heavily forested by immense trees, the hills drained at their bases by healthy creeks, appeared very similar to the Louisiana side of the Sabine. One subtle change was that the tall heavy pines began to thicken and in some places crowd out the more familiar hardwoods.

But the human environment had changed considerably. Even back at Gaines Ferry, the settlers and Jake and Two Hawks, too, had spoken at length with James Gaines after disembarking near the large sawn-board house that the ferry owner used as not only a residence but as an office and store as well. Gaines had introduced himself as both the ferry owner and the designated "Alcalde," a sort-of New Spain governor and captain, whose responsibility it was to keep track of who came and went, at least those he could find. Madame Dupre had produced correspondence that verified that the wagons were headed toward the lands set aside for the grant recipients of DeWitt's Colony, and that they were not bringing contraband of any kind, though the colonists did not learn what in fact was considered "contraband" by the Spanish authorities. They were all well aware that even runaway slaves were, if not welcomed, at least tolerated.

Early that afternoon, the wagons having stopped as two of the other teamsters helped Carpentier when his wagon mired and his mules wrenched free of the double-tree in a winding creek with two reddish sandbanks the Camino Real forded over, several of the travelers used the opportunity to readjust seating or harnesses, climbing down to stretch their legs. A few ladies discretely made their way into the side brush to care for their personal needs away from male eyes.

Black Drake laughed at some joke Peter had made and jumped down from the wagon, moving into the underbrush on the opposite side from where the females had entered. While that was a reassuring move to the rest of the men, who might have been concerned about the young Indian spying on their women at their toilette, Two Hawks quietly slipped down from his perch and hobbled off on the same north side, entering the underbrush at a different spot.

Knowing his element of stealth was diminished if not lost, Two Hawks determined to keep Black Drake in sight from behind the cover of a large Sweet Gum trunk, shifting then to the huge bark-plates of an immense Loblolly pine as the younger man dropped from view along the eroded creek bank.

A brief time later, he saw Black Drake climb out of the creek bed closer to the Camino, wipe his hands on his shirt, and start back toward the wagons. Nothing seemed amiss.

Still, after the young Caddo had worked his way through the underbrush and rejoined the wagons, Two Hawks swiftly hobbled/ shuffled over to the creek and retraced the young man's trail.

He found no signs of bodily evacuation, though close to where Black Drake had climbed back up out of the creek Two Hawks was startled by the still-writhing form of a headless snake, an example of the other's true namesake, which worried the old man. Though not a great believer in the ways of witches, he knew that frequently serious actions were spurred by the shaman's charms. The heavy body of a water moccasin lay at the base of the eroded clay. Jerking his hand back and chiding himself for carelessness, the old Caddo noted that a portion of the lighter underbelly of the snake gleamed in the bright moonlight. Looking closer, he bent and held out the headless form, the neck cleanly cut.

As the wagons rolled on that afternoon, Two Hawks thought about the still-writhing form of the heavy snake, drowned-man white and spackled with broken leaves, and his skin crawled. He must increase his vigilance, noting Black Drake's "stare" as he raised his head to the Dupre wagon in front of the team.

This part of the piney woods held a knife-sharp memory for Two

Hawks, as if even now slicing through his skin. As the wagons jostled along the Camino Real, he withdrew the memory and gazed into a gaping wound.

He had squatted in the shade of the sassafras tree, looked between delicate dewberry leaves to the thumb-sized lumps of rodent bones the owl had vomited from his perch. Mouse, young grey squirrel, and then, too, the delicate hollow bones that may have been from a passenger pigeon out for a last flight too close to evening.

And am I not an owl, too, Two Hawks had thought at the time, somewhat ironically with his bestowed name. Do I not often search and snatch my prey in the shadows, and vomit up their pieces I can't digest?

But he had avoided looking up, not wanting to find the owl with his eye, a bad omen that would be.

There to the south of the Neches River, near where the Spaniards' Camino Real had long been worn smooth with horses' hooves and the slapping soles of sandaled monks, the old Caddo had been sent for, once again to seek the truth where answers had been thus far, well, unsatisfactory. Two Hawks had been known to find the truth, was often not sought for that reason, too.

But a white man had been killed, gutted like a fish, the entrails of the living man wrapped around his legs.

Who would do such a thing, the runner had asked, a young Caddo with the lean shanks and torso of a long-distance hunter, as they wept quietly together in greeting, as was the tradition of their people, another tradition Two Hawks noted, that had slipped downstream in time. Two Hawks had not bothered to explain that *anyone* might do such a thing as this and much worse, did not bother because the innocence in the dark eyes of the young messenger had not space enough in his heart yet for such darkness.

Now *why* someone would do this thing was a more intriguing question, such questions that had served as Two Hawks' meat and drink.

Three white trappers with cabins near the village of Nacono had wasted no time in finding two Hasinai Caddo braves, each alone, and beaten them almost to death in an attempt to learn which Indian had committed the murder—to no avail. The Caddo knew nothing, and the elders had sent for Two Hawks to help.

But the bones in the owl's pellets had then, he recalled, brought to his mind the buffalo hunts, the lengths and lengths of intestine pulled from the still-quivering beasts, brought to the creek and cut into man-high lengths, under the running water squeezing out the bright-green half-digested spring grass, rinsing the pink tubes clean, to be later draped over roaring campfires, the intestines swelling, popping with grease and steam. These had been the feasts, the liver not even cooked but salted with a squeeze of buffalo urine from the bladder, the strong strips of flesh sliding down their young throats. Even then, those times were not to return.

He had to look at the body, the dead, the Indian having been there for two days and having not a single answer, no vision emerging of what had happened, and with whom.

The grave had been poorly marked with a broken plank from a wagon bed, the board a bright tan where the words had been cut: *Asa Clements, 24, kilt by Cadoos, 1807*. The surrounding woods leaned in, anxious to consume this bared patch of ground like a skinned knee.

Using a tin trade plate he had brought from the village, Two Hawks quickly scooped out the sandy reddish soil and decayed leaves until he felt the plate strike and slide off clothing. He then sat back on his heels and pulled a pouch around from behind his waist, taking out a sticky ball of fresh pine resin, rolling a small plug for each of his nostrils and a long roll to pack along the side of his tongue. The pungent smell of the resin, he had learned, would partly keep at bay the stench from the days'-old corpse.

No, they had not honored this man with one of the long wooden boxes the traders and Spaniards used to enclose their dead, still a mystery to the old Caddo. Why, with all their talk of their kind god and spirits, would one want to so trap a spirit or create any kind of impediment to that soul's wandering for another world?

And fortunately there had been no rain since before the last moon. The body slid easily from the still-loose earth, wrapped in sacking across the abdomen to hold in the intestines that had been so rudely removed. Two Hawks cut away the sacks with his trade knife, bit into the roll of resin in front of his tongue, and cut further into the swollen belly with a freshly knapped skinning tool he had created for the occasion, turning away at the rush of gas, suddenly staying his head in mid-turn at a shuffling in the dry hackberry leaves a spear's throw downwind. His ears gathered sound, quickly putting into bowls of memory the sounds of frog and cricket, armadillo and clumsy possum, leaving only the heavy crush of wide paws and that almost confused sound, not quite a cough or a snort or a chuckle, but that sound a black bear makes when he catches scent of what might be a meal.

"You go on, Bear!" Two Hawks had spoken loudly into the shadows. "Go, Bear. I am on your brother's business." He was bluffing, of course, but was gratified to hear the animal rush off in a snapping of twigs.

Asa Clements' small and large intestines, his stomach, revealed little: the remains of corn hulls and two or three grayish lumps still recognizable as salt pork in the fading glow of declining day told him little other than where he had taken his last meal.

But then the elder Caddo picked up each of the man's hands in turn. A man's hands told so much about him—how he worked, how careless, with what he had spent time. Asa's hands were trappers' hands, calloused on the first finger from guiding the blade under hides and around the joints, some stray cuts across the back of the other hand where a hasty swipe of a knife had moved too quickly, and he had the long thick nails that came in so handy in setting a sensitive trap or cracking body lice around the fire in the evening. His nails were full, Two Hawks saw, paring out deposits from each bed, the thick fat from fresh hides, bear grease for mosquitoes, dirt, and some yellow-orange ocher residue, all of which he carefully folded into a soft patch of sycamore bark and pouched.

In putting each hand down, though, the old man felt a stickiness on the hands, not sap or decay, and removing his nostril plugs for a moment breathed in the faint smell of that ribbon candy they sold at the trading post ...

After the sun had risen on the third day of his visit and he had completed his morning ablutions alone by a secluded creek, Two Hawks re-entered the Caddo village, squatting in the sun in front of the hive-shaped lodges, listening to the women talk of the growing corn and peppers, watching the lazy swing of their heavy breasts as they rubbed brains into the deerskins. A gaggle of young children laughed and played between the lodges, rolling a bois d'arc apple along with forked sticks.

"Did the trapper Asa Clements come to the village often?" Two Hawks had asked, and the women fell silent. One young woman looked away quickly and then down at her full breasts and her lap, covered by a doeskin wrap.

"He came sometimes," an old woman said. "He came and played with the children only, down by the river, talking to them, giving them sweet things from the post."

"Did he come to see anyone else?" And he pointedly looked at the young woman with the downcast eyes.

"No—the trapper was not interested in us," another woman spoke up, and tried to laugh, but the sound came out as a snort. No one else made a sound, and the music of the children's nearby play seemed to chide the women into their own thoughts.

Two Hawks noted one young boy of about three years whose lighter hair and skin spoke a story the old man heard but dimly and did not yet understand.

All those years before, with the sun directly over his head, Two Hawks had later stepped past the clearing in front of the Clements/ Jackson cabin to the brush and hide shelter of She-Ga, the earless Comanche woman who was fed and protected by the two trappers, or had been; in return, she had cleaned and cooked and did what other service the men required.

She brought out to him a clay bowl of beans and a rabbit haunch, brightened with spicy peppers, conveying in sign her cautious welcome, as they had already spoken two days before.

The old man had spoken in a combination of English, Caddo, a few words of Comanche, but mostly in sign, telling her that he knew about the village children and Clements' visits, about the candy and the light-skinned boy, asking if she knew about Clements' joining with the young Caddo woman. His eyes bored into the old woman's spirit, searching for truth.

After years of hard use and many beatings, She-Ga had so long worn an impassive mask that it was with an almost physical effort that her emotions of confusion and then a blaze of anger broke over her face and flared into her old eyes as she explained that the boy was not Clements' but Jackson's. Clements had other interests, she explained with disgust. She had one day followed him, reminding Two Hawks that even Comanche women knew how to stalk, to where the Caddo children played on the north bank of the Neches River, some watching his approach with fear, a few with wonder and excitement.

The woman made Two Hawks understand that Clements would give some of the children candy and they would let him touch their genitals and he would open his trousers and have them touch his. She said Clements never had any interest in her, even on lazy winter days. And the pale-skinned boy? Yes, she nodded, him too, even though he had just turned three, and she spat to either side of her, keeping back such bad medicine.

In the heat of the afternoon, Two Hawks had walked to the trading post and sat.

"Hey, old man, I hear a bear got into Asa's grave last night," said Tom Barkeley, the head of the post. He leaned back in his rough-hewn chair against the log wall of the storage building. "You know anything about that? Anything in the woods tell you about it?" A couple of local trappers chuckled at that, but Barkeley was intent upon the Indian's face—he had come to know that old Two Hawks saw more than most men, white or red.

"No, Long Tom," the Caddo said, seated on the beaten earth near the thick-planked door, but out of boot range. "The bears no longer speak to me."

Two men unloading sacks of parched corn snickered, and the old brave continued, "But did a bird tell me Asa Clements liked candy ...?" The question drifted out.

"Yeah," Barkeley said. "He bought so much of that hard ribbon candy I had to order more—how'd you know that, old one?"

"A bird, a dead bird, told me ..." He stopped and watched as Caleb Jackson stayed his hand on his mule's pack saddle. "Told me that Mister Clements liked the light ones the best—"

"Shut your mouth, you old bastard!" Jackson spun and shouted, fingers outstretched to grip the empty air. "Them birds tell you so damned much, they tell you who did for my partner, did they? Tell you it was me, did they?"

Two Hawks sat as though carved of stone; another man stopped his clay pipe half-way to his mouth.

"What are you all lookin' at? You know what he did, you must've know'd what he was doin'. I'm so darned stupid the old Comanch woman had to show me—with my own boy! Givin' him sweets and have that little boy touch his privates … Well, you're durned right, I caught 'im and he *lied*, said he was just playin'! I opened that old son quicker'n I'd do a deer, pulled out a loop, don't you see? Had to get him to confess to his Maker—his soul was going to his Maker, for sure, and he cryin' and beggin' me to stop, but he told me," Jackson said, with satisfaction and not a little madness. "He told God, and I slid that blade up under his ribs, looked into his red, wet piggy eyes and watched him go."

Caleb Jackson sat down in the sandy dirt right where he stood, and his shoulders began to tremble as the sobs worked over his frame.

The next morning, Two Hawks formally wept with Tsa' Bisu, the village healing doctor, as he gathered his pouches and slung his smooth-bore musket for departure, feeling deeply the welcome of his coming, and the joy at his leave-taking, too.

"No," he told the Caddo elders of the village, "they did not punish Caleb Jackson, but they would blame *you* no longer. He packed his mule with supplies and was told he must go toward the sun at day's end, beyond men's knowledge of this."

But Two Hawks told no one that Clements' belly had not been opened with a trapper's knife, remembering the young woman's doeskin skirt with the bright orange design visible in the fold. He had known, too, that at times the heart's stone can crush the soul to dust.

Chapter 28

In Jake Trap's wagon bed, Two Hawks had awoken well before dawn, the grasses and leaves pressing in upon the circle of wagons dripping with heavy dew. Having filled the iron water kettle the night before in preparation for his morning routine, and admittedly he liked the taste the iron added to the water whether this was imagined or not, he fed the embers of their dormant cookfire until it began to crackle to life, with tongues of yellow flame reaching the kettle that hung from the hook on the iron crossbrace.

Satisfied the fire would maintain itself for a time, he straightened with a groan and socketed his crutch once again under his right shoulder. The breaks in his lower leg were mending well, he could feel, but the stiffness in his back that came with the years took some minutes each morning to ease. That, and his shoulder joint pain and the occasional dull ache behind his left knee caused him to mutter audibly, "I should count which parts of me do *not* feel used up. But this earth has never promised me anything but change. And what is this ...?" Peter's bedding sheet and net were already empty and neatly folded.

Two Hawks quietly left camp and slid between bushes under the canopy of trees, noting with some satisfaction that the crutch/step/crutch rhythm had become an almost comfortable habit as he angled over toward a bend of Caballo Creek that would shield his morning ablutions from view, as was his habit.

Reaching a gently sloping bank, he approached the running water and pulled a strip of sassafras bark from his pouch, then scrubbed his teeth vigorously with the bark to chase the morning taste. With some satisfaction he found that he still heard the trembling of vines behind him as he bent over the eddying pool of the creek where he had chosen to wash, bending to rinse and seeing the reflection in the quiet water.

"Well, Snake, how much longer will you wait?"

"No longer, old man," the young Indian said. He stepped onto the sandbar near where Two Hawks stood. "Too many eyes are growing up around us, so I must proceed. Know I will kill Peter and Madame, too, but, contrary to my wishes, you will not live to see those two suffer. But do not concern yourself—I will tell them who set their deaths in motion."

"You would take me down here, boy?"

Snake laughed. "Yes, a snake will take you down." He opened his hand to reveal the head of the water moccasin from the preceding day. "Even after they die, snakes can bite," he said. "And as you suffer with the poison and you say crazy things about my using a snake's head to bite you, no one will believe you. 'How sad—the doddering fantasies of the old man!'"

Laughing, suddenly Snake's foot lashed forward, sweeping Two Hawks' crutch out from under him in the soft sand, the old Caddo going down to one knee as his attacker sprang forward, the cottonmouth's head upraised.

Snake's arm sweeping down, he froze in mid-motion and looked down at the soiled front of his French shirt, to where the wet point of a steel arrowhead protruded. The question in his eyes faded as his heart, lacerated by the blades of the steel point, beat its last rush of blood into his chest, and he fell forward, sliding off Two Hawks' upraised arm.

Peter emerged from the brush behind the sandbank, bow in hand. He looked down at where the young Caddo sprawled in the sand, the stench of fresh blood and emptied bowels welling out from the still form.

"Two Hawks—he would have killed you!"

"Yes, Peter," said Two Hawks, seeing the look of distress on the boy's face. "You and your mother, too. You were close enough to hear—you did what you needed to do."

Peter just stood and stared into the twisted face of Snake that had driven itself into the sand. Full minutes later, he finally rasped, "But is it always like—this killing someone? The empty feeling?"

"No, young son, he died quickly. At times they die more slowly, grab you, or stare into your eyes and want desperately to take you with them. But however it happens, or why, regardless of the need, it is the same in one way ..." His voice and eyes drove into the distance.

"How the same?" Peter was feeling the weight, the burden of what had been done.

"You know, Peter—you know. You will never be the same. This man had lived, however badly or hatefully or wrongfully, for a number of seasons, and now he has no more. You took from him what he knew and felt or would ever know or feel or change into or be—yes, son, let the tears come for most of us, it is always something terrible to end a life, even when you must."

"But he—" Peter began.

"But we both know, yes, you took the true action, and I thank you for saving these old bones," Two Hawks said, creasing his eyes in a kind smile.

And the moment was released, like a cast iron lid coming off a bubbling stew, for the present at least.

Peter stepped over and nudged the snake head with his boot: "How could he use this?"

Two Hawks rolled into a sitting position and picked up the wide head of the cottonmouth, gripping the skinned stalk of neck immediately behind the head in one hand and pulled the skin forward off the top of the skull, aiming it toward a fallen log. The mouth of the water moccasin gaped, the two half-inch fangs surrounded at their bases by still swollen white flesh sprang forward, and two jets of venom sparkled an arm's length in the morning sun before darkening the grey wood of the dried log.

"Before we grew into men," Two Hawks said, "we played some dangerous jokes and game. The skin's pressure on the poison bags squeezes them." He dropped the head to the sand. Looking up, he said, "That bow—we made that a handful of seasons ago. You brought it ..." This time the eyes of the old Caddo swam.

"Of course, Two Hawks—I could never forget what we have done. I am sorry I borrowed a few of your special arrows you had Corey make, but I went out this morning to bring a deer back for the pot, wanted to use one of your arrows so you could be with me."

"And I was not far away, Peter—in my thoughts I will always be with you and your mother—but soon we will be missed and we have work to do. Help me pull Snake beneath those grape vines. Then we will wash this blood from the sand—"

"What do you mean? We need to tell everyone you were right about him, that he—"

"That he what, Peter? Tried to bite me with a dead snake's head? And then? Even if they all believe us, which I doubt, and let us bury him here, someone will tell the authorities, somewhere, people will look at you differently..."

"Then *what*? We cannot simply drag him under a bush and leave him here, for the animals!"

"Large or small, Peter, the animals always have us, and then the earth. Folks at the wagons saw Snake leave, saw me leave—we will tell them I saw him take my pouch of coins, and you, out hunting, heard my confrontation and joined us. He confessed, since we found the pouch beneath his shirt after a short struggle, and he agreed to leave. He will not be back—another thieving Indian," Two Hawks added with a smirk.

"But someone will find him—"

"Long after we have moved on. Now lend a hand—this crutch does not make lifting a simple task ..."

Grasping Snake under the arms, the limp head rolling back, Peter was discomfited by how very heavy the weight of the dead man was, as Two Hawks put his left arm under the limp knees of the body and helped Peter angle up the creek bank toward the thick mound of vines covering a fallen tree. He and Peter were quickly bathed in sweat from the effort but began to roll the corpse under the wide leaves. Two Hawks braced himself with his crutch and put his moccasined foot firmly on Snake's back next to the arrow shaft's entry, broke off the willow shaft and withdrew the remainder of the shaft with the steel arrowhead from the front.

"We do not want anyone coming upon the carcass to have too much to think about," he said. He and Peter then returned to the sandbank and scooped water up onto the sand to dissipate the clotting blood, the younger man clearly disturbed by the blood touching his fingers as he washed.

Chapter 29

Ambling slowly back toward the road, the two wanted to provide time for their perspiration to dry, Two Hawks slowly tearing the arrow shaft's fletching into small pieces and snapping the shaft several times before cutting off the rinsed steel point and packing it away into his pouch. Peter watched through sidelong glances and wondered at the old Caddo's calm demeanor, his steady fingers, wondered how many other times Two Hawks might have accomplished similar obfuscations.

"Remember, Peter ..." Two Hawks' calm undisturbed voice shocked Peter more profoundly than would have tears or shouts. "We discovered a thief in our camp and sent him on his way. That is the truth. Snake sought to steal from me everything I hold close, your mother, and you not least. But I understand that you will need to tell Madame what has taken place this day—present it to her when you must." She will understand that the earth has changed for us all, Two Hawks thought.

Shortly after Jake Trap and Two Hawks had chewed through a noon repast of dried pears, jerked venison, and some fry bread while the wagons rolled west, Trap flicked the loose rein across the mare's rump, killing a horsefly in a satisfying spot of blood, saying, "So, Hawks," beginning to abbreviate the Caddo's name in a manner the Indian was as yet undecided about, "you going to tell me the truth of this morning? I know for a fact your coin pouch never left camp, and that boy up in that wagon there looks like he sees Caesar's ghost."

"Not seen a ghost," Two Hawks answered. "Made one. He killed Snake as that man was moving to strike."

"Snake tried to kill Peter?"

"No, not yet. Snake was very close to finishing my journey," and Two Hawks spent some minutes telling the trapper what had taken place, and what the two had done afterward.

Jake looked off over the heads of the wagon team, looked back over a vale of years, before saying, "That first one is bad, if you see the body up close after he's gone, if you are a thinking man."

After Attoyac Bayou, as the Camino, or the Old San Antonio Road, was increasingly called out here, wound its way almost due west, the miles unreeled beneath the wagon beds like an errant spool of woolen thread fallen from a basket. The towering pines provided thick shade, their fallen needles cushioning the trail, at times the only sounds hushed clicks from drivers' mouths to keep the teams moving and occasional rattle of trace chains. Creeks were running in moderation, and the wagon group passed through Nacogdoches without incident, stopping only at the house of the governor, Antonio Gil Ibarro, to gather news of the road ahead and peruse several maps. They quickly moved on, feeling without speaking it that they were meant to do this, and they did not wish to disturb the motion forward.

What they learned caused both trepidation and hope. Bands of Comanche and Kiowa, it seemed, continued to raid and harass travelers on the south fork of the Camino, known as the La Bahia Road, but a settlement and fortified outpost called La Grange had recently been established by colonists of an American empresario where the road crossed the Colorado River. Further south, where Martin DeLeon had finally obtained permission to bring in Mexican settlers on the Guadalupe River, near DeWitt's colony, he had platted a new town called Victoria, which would be a welcome source of supplies and company once the settlers began to build.

Fording the Angelina River in a spotty spring shower early in the day, the colonists decided to push on quickly until they reached a grassy area some twenty miles west where there had been no recent rain but near the banks of the Neches River. Wood was quickly gathered and cookfires ablaze in the gloaming, and Two Hawks, with a solemnity seldom seen in recent days, hobbling a little less each day, made his way over to where Peter and Jake worked on the worn hames of the Dupre harnesses.

He touched the shoulder of each gently and said, "Come."

The word was spoken so gravely that the two simply put down the leather pieces they had been employed with and stood, glanced quickly at each other, and followed the old Caddo's retreating back.

Obviously Two Hawks expected them to follow and had no inclination to explain. The three were soon swallowed by the underbrush of a hardwood copse south of the trail, but Jake and Peter were then surprised some moments later at the sudden rise in the forest floor, a small steep hill looming almost as a wall before them in the fading light. They could just make out an even larger mound rising through the tree trunks further south.

Two Hawks had seated himself on a large fallen sycamore trunk, his stick crutch now polished with use leaning beside him.

"Perhaps there is purpose in all things," he began, and looked up at his two companions. Jake had been about to make a remark about the old Indian sounding like some biblical prophet again, but he swallowed his gibe on seeing the other's expression.

Peter knew Two Hawks well enough to recognize the time to be still—and listen.

Chapter 30

"These were my people, the old Caddo, before now, before the French and the Spanish, before the new corn ..." His voice seemed to drift up through the new leaves like a smoke, and he reached down at his feet, scooping up a handful of acorns and sycamore burrs from beneath the detritus. "The seeds of time fall all around us, some gathered, some eaten, many fall unseen. This is the home of my people, and we will never be here again."

Peter's eyes filled with the image passed to him and said, "We can if we want," but he knew as soon as the words were out that he spoke a wish of youth, and his seemed to be swiftly draining away like corn meal through loose fingers.

Jake was sad for the boy, not ever a boy again, really, but Peter was fighting both backward and forward, wanting to keep the world as it was but being inexorably propelled forward, by Snake, by the looks of a dangerous woman, the young Eudice Carpentier—Jake had seen the looks cast Peter's way, seen the confused flush on his face, followed by an awkward almost-rooster strut. The old trapper had caught, too, John Carpentier's dark look at least once as well, and knew a mess of trouble would be dished out on more than one plate in the weeks ahead.

As if reading Jake's thoughts, Two Hawks caught the other's long look, the two old men understood without speaking that their paths, too, would soon diverge and be lost in the mist.

"Talked to a old mountain man a few months back. Name of Antony Glass, told me about a trail he cut west of here, yonder," he said, and pointed, and "yonder" sounded to Peter as far away as the moon. Peter also did not understand that, for such men, "cutting a trail" just meant they had walked or rode that way. But they all knew Trap was announcing his intention to leave the group, how soon the other two did not know.

"You going with him, Two Hawks?" Peter tried to sound casual and trail-hardened, but his voice cracked.

Two Hawks instead looked south, past the mounds and the trees, to a yonder that was kept from his companions. "Not yet, young sir." His eyes creased suddenly into what Peter recognized as one of his old smiles, and the solemnity was broken as sharply as the snapping of a twig.

Peter had momentarily been confused at the distance the formal sound of "young sir" seemed to put between them, but then looking at Jake, the realization grew upon him that his childhood friend and, well, his sometime guardian, was calling Peter a man. He swelled briefly with a newfound pride before feeling the temper of an infinite sadness, as when a forged blade is suddenly thrust into the chill water. But he lifted his chin and rose.

"I need to help Mother with the camp," he announced, somewhat alarmed that he had made this decision without waiting for the others to move first.

Three days later, the hills gradually beginning to lengthen, the oaks growing shorter as the wagons rolled west, the trail forded the Trinity River in the afternoon light, and the teams were unharnessed, the wagons having been drawn into a rectangle for security. Women and children walked back to the riverbank to collect driftwood for cookfires, and the men leaned on wagon gates, smoking cob pipes and discussing the road ahead, repairs that had presented themselves, and dreams that were finding fertile soil in the country around them.

Chapter 31

Two Hawks and Jake Trap's nostrils flared, smelled the band before the lead Kiowa walked openly toward the wagons as the sun began to fall toward the long hills stretching out to the west. The scent of woodsmoke and animal fat had reached the Caddo several moments ago, so he knew the Indians had been watching the wagons' inhabitants for some time before deciding on an approach.

Startled, Peter lunged for his musket, but Two Hawks and Jake both calmed him with backstretched arms. The old trapper spoke quietly, not taking his eyes or smile off the lead Kiowa: "Be calm, young son. They wanted to, you would be dead already, or squirming on the ground. They'd of hit us from the trees and only come in to finish."

Peter leaned his rifle on the wagonbed, embarrassed but trying to look casual. Two Hawks limped carefully forward, his crutch left propped against a wheel. The older Kiowa, others spread among the underbrush behind, walked forward through the dry leaves and branches, making no sound but looking at the native before him with mild confusion and consternation, before beginning in a mixture of sign and Kiowa and Spanish: "An important but broken old Caddo you appear, but why with these town whites that look to take land?"

"Your eyes are old but see more than young eyes," Two Hawks began, sensing that the Kiowa was more curious than dangerous, and the Caddo explained their situation, reassuring the other man that while he was correct on both counts, the wagons were heading far to the south, many days travel from these Kiowa lands—while he spoke he could not keep from staring at the Kiowa's tiny and delicate nose, almost like a child's, wondering as he had many times before why the Kiowa as a group had such small noses, where they had come from, long before now. He slowly reached into his pouch and brought out a large pinch of pemmican, passing half to the Kiowa before putting the rest into his mouth and beginning to chew as he finished speaking.

The other Indian slowly chewed and nodded in appreciation, then speaking over his shoulder to the others in the band. A young brave, his powerful leg muscles shining with fat as he moved, strode forward with a large haunch of a mule deer over his shoulder, then swinging the meat effortlessly down to rest it near Two Hawks' moccasin before melting back into the woods without a glance.

Several minutes later, the parley over, the Kiowas were gone, their scent soon lost in the growing shadows.

Limping back to the wagons and the others' questioning looks, Two Hawks thought of something else the Kiowa had said. He spoke to the settlers: "That Kiowa means no harm, and most Kiowa are the same, but their brothers, the Comanche, are not so minded. He told me we are entering the lands of the Comanche, where they do as they wish, the land the Spanish call the 'Comancheria,' so our vigilance must be constant."

The next morning, and in the days that followed, the men kept their muskets next to them on the drivers' benches and near at hand as they camped. The women, too, those who had no muskets of their own, chatted less and kept kitchen knives, even cast iron pans, near at hand, having heard the stories of how the Comanche often did not kill the women ...

A few days later, having then forded the Navasota River and seeing a wide plain to the west heavily peppered with dead dwarf cedars that resolved themselves into a small herd of buffalo, Jake looked at the blue distance and said, "I'll be pulling out at first light."

Two Hawks looked in that direction as well. "Keep your skin tight, Jake Trap. Those Comanche, Apache, too, as you know enjoy testing a man, seeing what he is made of, by looking underneath ..."

They both set camp especially carefully that evening, as if reminding themselves and each other the kind of men they had been travelling with, their work concluded by wrapping Trap's doubletree chains in strips of still-green deer hide from the Kiowas' haunch.

Peter thought he knew the answer but asked nonetheless: "That to keep the chains quiet?"

Continuing his work, Jake said, "I need all the luck I can get, or make, and the sound of those steel links is like nothing natural," and all three men stopped and thought about all that he suggested with those words.

Though Two Hawks had awoken before first light, with the initial groan of the wagonbed as Jake began his descent to the ground to begin harnessing, others in camp only stirred when the spotted mare complained at the collar's weight this early, by which time the trapper had already begun to turn his wagon out of the box formation.

Trap finally turned to the old Caddo and gripped his forearm tightly before the other drew him close in a full embrace.

Two Hawks' tattooed cheeks were wet with tears, as he knew that this white man had propelled one footfall that led to another and another until three people, one red and two white, had been pulled from a precipice of another's making. And they both cast backward their memories to the time when Caddo met and departed from each other with tears, both a custom and a manner of feeling now lost—lost.

Chapter 32

Later that day, Two Hawks jostling along behind the seat of the Dupres' wagon, Peter with the reins wondered aloud at the brace of nearly new animal traps the old man had left in their wagon.

"He will get more," Two Hawks said, "when he reaches the settlement called Santa Fe, in the far mountains. Not much use for many traps until then, not many beaver for days and days, moons, he thinks."

And it was relatively easy travel for the wagons rolling more pointedly south for the next two weeks, the settlers encountering no one except a handful of mounted Comanche after the wagons had rattled and rocked across a deep ford on the Brazos after dawn, but the meeting had been tense.

Though the spring had been warm, a chill had remained in the early morning air, seemed to pool as a mist close to the ground, the four mounted Comanche on the nearby bluff wearing nothing but scant leather breechclouts. Two carried bows and quivers strapped to their backs, one a bit older held a trade musket, but the obvious leader, mounted on a solid grey mustang emblazoned by two crimson handprints on his withers and held in a motionless stand by a horsehair hackamore, this older Comanche casually held a different musket draped over his arm, the stock and lock elaborately engraved and chased in silver.

He saw the eyes of the teamsters and others settle on the beautiful gun and he smiled very slowly when they raised their looks to his bronze face.

Tossing the musket suddenly up into the air before him, the brave snatched it mid-stock as it fell and thrust it over its head, piercing the still air with a screeched war cry, followed by cries from the other three. None of the horsemen, however, moved their legs or mounts.

The wagons had been stopped since the first appearance of the Indian group, the Anglo men now nervously holding their guns, but Jake Trap and Two Hawks had been schooling the group for some time, and the settlers attempted to look confident but unmoved by the Comanches' display while making their weapons clearly visible.

In an instant, the Indians wheeled their horses as one and were gone, the bluff where they had sat their ponies empty in the blue western sky.

Later in camp, the men except for a lookout gathered around the Dupres' cookfire, Will Logan asking Two Hawks what he thought of the encounter. The men were feeling especially uneasy now that Jake Trap had gone, and quite frankly they needed some reassurance they had handled the situation with appropriate aplomb, and that this Indian, Two Hawks, now far from civilization, was in fact a part of their purpose.

"The Comanche were not sure," Two Hawks began, "that they had enough to make easy work of you. Remain on guard, as they may easily return with others, though we do not know how far from the main group they had come."

"Where'd that lead one get that rifle he was tossing around?" Caleb Samuels sounded a bit angry but mostly uncomfortable. He himself suspected the answer.

"Oh, he wanted us to see that weapon. Wanted us to know well it came from the hand of a dead man." Two Hawks smiled for a moment and let it slide from his face, reading the other men's thoughts, knowing that white men did not trade such muskets to red men.

And what settled in on the men around the fire, like heavy hands that then seemed to reach right down through their coats and into their chests, gripping their hearts, was the realization for the first time, for some the first time in their lives, that this was not their land. Not like the land back in Louisiana, where even if the land did not belong to them,

126

those other miles and miles and hectacre after hectacre of forest and field others had deed or possession of, the country, was still *their* country. Oh, there were some loose bands and tatters of Indians still wandering in it, but Louisiana was white man's land, part of some grand design, they knew.

These four Comanches had told them with their presence, their dramatic confidence, that this was different. This was Comancheria, and this small train of wagons and women and children were vulnerable strangers, like a small herd of whitetails slipping past napping wolves, trying to get south before dying in ways they did not even want to imagine.

"You did well this morning." Two Hawks nodded gravely. "You will get where you are going."

The others bobbed their heads in return, feeling a bit more confident, more secure, though a couple of older men thought about the Caddo's words and realized he had provided scant reassurance. We will all get where we are going, they thought—always.

Two Hawks smiled to himself slowly as he turned and limped toward the wagon, and wondered if any of these men gathered here would come to realize the position they now shared with him, the aloneness, since he had lived as a stranger under suspicion most of his adult life, a Caddo in lands he knew were no longer Caddo, frequently the object of hostile observation. The table were turned now, at least for these people who had abandoned the comfort of the known.

Chapter 33

Several days later, the wooded hills gently descended in what the settlers assumed was a sizeable watercourse, and the meandering growth of larger trees roughly north and south some two days south of what they took to be Yegua Creek, if the maps they had pored over in Nacogdoches were correct, meant this was the Colorado River, meant, too, that they were perhaps only a week or two from their destination.

Two Hawks, not having made a point of studying the worn parchment of the Spanish map they had been permitted to access in Nacogdoches, had stared past their intent murmuring and pointing fingers to where this river they now approached wound its way like a length of unraveled yarn to the big water, what they called the Gulf of Mexico, the river emptying north of a large bay he had recognized from his earlier travels. He knew he would leave the wagons at the Colorado.

Considerable white smoke was seen threading up from a stand of oaks as the wagons slowly rolled toward the river and a collection of cabins and storage barns close to mid-day. Near a pile of stones and powdered rubble outside a large makeshift oven in the open air, two men stopped their shoveling of burned stone from the kiln's iron door. The transformed limestone would be mixed into mortar for more permanent structures, the settlers thought.

"Welcome to La Grange!" A short balding man behind a plank counter in the "General Merchandise" cabin looked up from two racks of colored thread he had been arranging and grinned at the wagoners as they filed in. His grin was swept off as his evaluation of the group reached the darkly tattooed Caddo he saw through the open door.

Two Hawks did not think the man's welcome extended to him, but he felt no resentment, suspecting in this part of the country that most Indians looked like Comanche to most whites.

"La Grange ..." Will said, trailing off.

"Yes, sir, named for Chatoo de la Grange-Blenoo, French place of Lafayeete, helped us in the War of Independence. We have a cultivated ford for the Colorado River, some streets plotted out, working on a stone fort just north, had more than a bit of trouble with the Comanch—" The words had spilled out of him, sensing some new customers, until he stopped himself and stared out at Two Hawks leaning against the wheel brake outside, slowly scratching his back on the wheel's iron rim.

Peter followed the direction of the storekeeper's stare. "He's Caddo. No better man at your side." The other men nodded in acknowledgement.

"You say so. Name's Abe Thomason. Where you folks headed? Though there's not much better than right here—"

"Guadaloopee River," Will said. "Going to join DeWitt's. You hear any news of down there?"

"Matter of fact—appears Dewitt and DeLeon do not like rubbing shoulders with each other too much, from what I hear. Might step careful—that new Mex gov'mint does change its mind." The storekeeper looked over their heads into what might have been the future.

"Will you help old Two Hawks one more time?" The Caddo looked at Peter as they finished their morning tea, leaning their backs against a storage trunk they had removed to rearrange the load in the deep wagonbed. Two Hawks' sudden seriousness was a bit disconcerting.

"Anything in the world I can do." Peter somehow sensed this presaged a shift in his world.

"I saw a small boat, what the French call a bateau or pirogue, pulled up on the rocks next to the bank," and Two Hawks saw the mouth and eyes of Peter Hayes draw tight. "It is time, young son, to leave you and your mother to your new future; my journey leads to this river's end. No, do not protest—my spirit feels heavy as a fish at the end of a line. I might follow the river along the banks, usually simple enough, but with my leg not completely healed as new, a float down the river, well, as it lasts might be a better choice—here, if you will, take this coin and buy the boat for me, if the man will sell. They might honor the sale more with you."

"This is *gold*, Two Hawks. Too much," said Peter as he hefted the weight of the coin in his hand. "Permit me." He rose and stepped back over to the tool box fixed to the outside of the wagon bed. Taking tongs, a cold chisel, and a hammer, he made quick work of cutting off a third of the coin, passing the remainder back to his still-seated friend.

Two Hawks nodded approval. "Your time helping Samuel Corey was well spent."

"We do not want these folks to think we have money to waste," Peter added, and busied himself with stowing the cups to avoid dwelling on Two Hawks' words.

The Caddo levered himself into standing, and while he had made no sounds, his clenched jaw was ample witness to the pain he still felt in his mending leg.

Early as it was, the sun not yet sending its medicinable eye through the oaks east of the river, the two made their way out of camp and into the cluster of dwellings called La Grange, the sounds of hammer on steel ringing out from the smith shop, an early start to avoid the combination of the forge's heat and the heat of the day.

"These are your sounds, Peter," said Two Hawks. "Yours and your mother's, too, the signs of 'progress,' as they say, the signs of new."

"There is a place for you, old friend," Peter said. "Always with us there is a place for you."

"And I believe you, young man, I will always have a place with you, and that is a pleasure to keep. But there is no time for me ..." He thought about trying to explain that something new for someone was something old for someone else, something gained for one is something lost for another. And he thought about this thing, almost a being, these new people called "time," but even they were only new here. They were old where they came from, they had repeatedly told him, so many old that they came here to be new. And he was one of the old already here, but all this was just words, he thought, because he had come to know that what is new is always old, and the beginning was always the end and the end the beginning. Time, they said, moved forward, but he knew better, that time was just another way some people tried to *count* what could only be counted in relation to themselves. He knew Peter could not yet understand, so he kept silent.

Chapter 34

Once the two found the boat's owner, an aging German named Hans Schlegel (Two Hawks enjoyed pronouncing the man's last name over and over, feeling his mouth shaping the new sounds), Peter and Mr. Schlegel settled on a price, the latter somewhat regretfully as he had spent many a pleasant hour, he said, crafting the vessel, after which Peter passed over the cut piece of the gold coin and brought out a tight roll of parchment no larger than his hand.

"And let us make out a proper bill of sale," Peter said, having been carefully instructed by Two Hawks as they had walked to town.

"Ya," said Hans, "goot to know where tings come from." He quickly wet a quill and wrote out what Peter suggested, adding, "Permit me to provide you with a paddle and a supply of oakum. I will have no use for them now. I made dat boot as well as I can, but like old man it can leak sometimes," and he chuckled at his own joke.

After passing back over to the west bank of the Colorado with the boat in tow, Peter and Two Hawks, back at the wagon, freshened a turkey quill and then adjusted the bill of sale, signing the boat over to the old

Caddo. He understood that some Europeans had difficulty accepting Indian ownership of anything, and the parchment might serve a purpose.

"So, you will leave us again?" Margaret Dupre watched as Two Hawks made final adjustments to his kit, including a small oilskin satchel Peter had presented him with, well-packed with dried peaches and pears and a cast lead soldier the boy had had since he was four years old. Peter had held onto it over a series of successive moves, he wasn't sure why, but he knew he needed to let it go, this last vestige of childhood, but wanted his friend to have it. "You can melt it down or hammer it into a musket ball if you have a need," he had said, but Two Hawks knew the value Peter had placed on the talisman.

And while the young man did not wish it this way, he had embraced the old Indian in camp, with manly claps on the back, watching as Two Hawks and Margaret Dupre stepped down the path to the river alone.

Looking at but not seeing the small boat as it tugged gently at a hemp painter in the quiet eddy behind a fallen cottonwood trunk, Margaret spoke: "I knew it would come to this, knew it was for the best, but I would at present wish you would remain with us, Two Hawks. Do not leave us. A new place, a new life," she said, reaching back to place a hand on his upper arm.

Two Hawks, too, made the pretense of watching the boat. Both of them were concerned of what might occur if they looked at each other now.

"Madame Dupre—" he began.

"Stop it!" She spoke sharply, knowing that he wished the distance. "Two Hawks, let us depart as we are."

And the two turned and embraced, Margaret openly weeping and the old Caddo's eyes simply running.

After some minutes, both of their minds running like fresh streams with memories and, yes, possibilities, he finally stood back and cleared his throat, in part embarrassed at old physical awakenings, too.

"We two know, Margaret Dupre, it is the fear of what is to come, known and unknown, that brings thoughts of what cannot come to pass."

"Were it a different world ..." Her eyes brimmed again.

"Always the same world," he said, repeating. "Always the same world, over and over. Only we are briefly different."

"Oh, damned world." Margaret Dupre reached into the folds of her skirt, to the small pocket sewn into it, withdrew a tiny object and pressed it into his palm, turning away and walking back up the path without looking back. She stopped for just a moment to glare at two townswomen across the river.

He watched until her form was obscured by the undergrowth before opening his hand. The gold heart, no larger than his smallest fingernail, without any hole or ring to attach it to anything, shone up at him, and he understood that the responsibility was his to keep it secured.

Chapter 35

He untied the mooring painter and carefully stepped into the boat and settled himself on the oak seat, picking up his worn crutch. Although he no longer needed it to walk, he had kept it in the wagonbed, deciding that the seasoned limb would serve well to pole the boat out of shallows and away from large stones or deadfalls. He would save the artfully shaped paddle blade for making headway or steering through the swift broad expanses to come as the river deepened near the mouth.

As the sun rose warmer in the bright southern sky, the boat drifted, bobbed, and spun its way down the broad expanse of the river, the water's rich earth tones and milky jade greens threading through deep currents. The banks were often bristling with drifted branches and limbs looking like mendicants reaching out for alms.

Having adjusted his scant belongings along the thwarts and beneath the seat, the interior of the hull as yet clean and dry, Two Hawks tentatively dipped the paddle into the flowing water, turning the wooden blade this way and that, feeling the craft respond and taking stock of changes in direction.

He recalled numbers of keelboats on the lower reaches of the Rive Rouge, the steersmen up on platforms at the sterns, long rough-hewn tillers in their hands directing the deep plank rudders, and he resolved to experiment with that idea.

As the sun began its descent later that day, the boat making considerable distance, though not without frequent bailing, his old tin teacup finding new employment, he had rounded yet another broad bend with no groundings. Steering with the paddle held in the water tightly at his side, he kept toward the cutbank and deeper water, deciding to look for a reasonable landing.

The shadows lengthened on a long straight reach, thickly wooded banks evenly carved on both sides, and Two Hawks saw at a distance what appeared to be a cloud of black and white and brown rags surging across the river.

"Horses," he whispered aloud. "Mustangs, must be two hands full," and his tiny craft drifted swiftly towards the wild herd swimming and churning toward the east bank, where the animals clamored up onto a sandbank and shook before charging into the underbrush near where a creek delivered its freight to the larger stream.

Two Hawks aimed his boat for the spot, dwelling on the memory of what he had seen, the wild rolling whites of the horses' eyes in their abandon, the stallion nipping playfully but with purpose at his mares, keeping them together, driving them from the vulnerable open ground into the protection of the trees, the spots and random patterns of colors on their wet coats ablaze with the years of wild breeding beyond the reach of meddling human habitation.

The landing would serve as a good camp as well, the wild herd not favoring areas that were settled or cultivated.

He grounded the boat on the long finger of sandbank reaching into the river on the south entrance of the creek, removed his moccasins, and stepped into the cold spring flow, using the bowline to pull his craft to the main bank and well up onto the shore, securing the painter to an exposed root. He took no chances, knowing that a strong spring rain to the north could easily raise the water level several arms deep as he slept.

Though the ground was well pocked with the hooves of wild horses, suggesting that this was indeed a secure spot for a lone traveler, Two Hawks nonetheless resolved to make his first landing a cold camp, finding an immense old oak claiming an entire clearing nearby, its ancient branches reaching out and, of their own weight, resting on the sandy ground some five or six man-lengths from the central trunk.

Understanding an accessibility that permitted other animals, four-legged and two, the same easy path, Two Hawks shifted and balanced his pouches, slung his musket tightly to his back and waddled slowly up along a heavy limb lush with moss and fern. Reaching the branch's joint with the main trunk, he propped his rifle against the rough bark, charged the barrel with powder, patch and shot, and affixed the nipple with a percussion cap, the hammer at half-cock, draping a leather patch over the barrel's muzzle to keep out a stray rain shower before settling in for the night.

The hollow crotch of limb and trunk was littered with small bird and rodent bones, obviously a frequently improvised table for a hawk or wildcat. The Caddo did not disturb the tiny bones but instead covered them with bright green moss before comfortably seating himself with his back to the main part of the tree, from which he noted with satisfaction he could just make out the bow and securing line of the bateau tied up. While he knew that were his leg completely recovered, if it ever would be, he might have found a better perch higher up, he knew that at least water moccasins and heavier rattlesnakes and copperheads would avoid even this modest height in a tree. And then amid the gathering sounds and furtive movements of falling darkness, his eyes closed and he was asleep.

Chapter 36

A piece of dead twig dropped onto the back of his bare hand, and Two Hawks opened his eyes without stirring in the rosy dawn, listening to the delicate patter of discarded stems and leaves around him. He did not need to look up to recognize a squirrel's early frenetic activity. "Well, old friend," he said, "if you're awake, your carelessness seems aimed at making sure the rest of the world is awake, too."

He wondered, not for the first time, if this is how his world might end, or at least this round of it, that in some isolated old tree such as this, one morning he would simply not open his eyes to the hurled irritations of a distracted squirrel, he would just dry up or even rot, unseen and undisturbed, until his bones, the skin at last melting off, his bones might become the toys of bored raccoon kits ... not such a distasteful close.

"Well, not yet," he said aloud, and chewed on half a handful of dried peach and pecan meats packed together with beef fat and boucan.

A faint mist softened the surface of the river to the north as he sat on a drifted trunk next to his tethered boat ready for launching. Looking at the practicality of the paddle's design, including a securely mortised t-handle for a sound handhold, he then found an arm's length drifted limb sanded smooth by running water and fixed it crosswise to the paddle with rawhide laces from his hunting vest. The result was a workable rudder and accompanying tiller that would reach the oak thwart-seat.

Two Hawks had appreciated the long narrow keel-strip the old German had affixed to the hull's bottom to keep lee-slide to a minimum, and he now used his knife to pry up the narrow board far enough to get a longer lace in front of the last securing nail, adding another lace at the upper rail. While he had thus lost the rawhide strap of one of his pouches, the newly fashioned steering assembly was now secured at two points, and swiveled with relative ease.

As he attempted to push off into the current, though, he felt the paddle blade grind into the gritty mud of the bottom with his weight, and he slumped back onto the seat with a sigh.

Oh, but the old Caddo was tired, he thought to himself, tired of challenge, setting his wits against the amorphous fog of this so often wicked world. "Perhaps I should go with them," he said aloud, thinking about the contentment of sitting on the edge of Madame Dupre's porch, watching the colors of the setting sun, wrapped in the secure and reliant affection of Margaret and her son, at least until she found another man, which would be in her best interest to do, and until Peter found a woman reasonable enough to keep him on a path. Their neighbors and the village folk would have theories, of course, resentments and suspicions, he secretly hoped would be well-founded. And he could forget this foolishness that was his current quest and catch them, perhaps even reach the coast, move south along it and rejoin them by making his way up the Guadaloupe ...

And be the tired old Indian on the farm, maybe whittle some toy bows and arrows, pretend not to hear the comments, the open stares from those who knew nothing about what he had been, "Like a dried-up old bull, content."

He visibly shook off the images, pushed the boat around until the deeper blade of the rudder was free in the current, reseated himself and pushed off stern-first, feeling the swift water pull him from the safety of the bank.

Twice he grounded that day on un-suspected mud or sandbanks, finding the rudder difficult to disengage as the small boat pirouetted around it in the currents, but Two Hawks found considerable pleasure in the ability to roughly steer and navigate that the paddle gave him.

At times, when the banks narrowed between limestone bluffs and the volume of murky water broke over submerged shelves and swirled around fists of undissolved stone, he could see in his mind's eye what might occur if the boat were to turn abeam in the swift current and strike an obstruction, how the wall of water would mount almost instantly on the upstream side of the hull and flip it over, spilling him and his supplies. And were he able to recover the craft and his supplies, quite a feat in itself, much of his powder and perhaps even the delicate percussion caps would become damp and useless.

But he learned a great deal about steering that day, shipping several gouts of water on occasion but avoiding any major mishap. Seeing the banks slip by even faster than a horse trot, he knew that his decision to procure the boat had been a sound one. Again that day, while several times passing what were obvious fords and once taking note of the bloated carcass of a calf snagged on a submerged tree, he saw no human inhabitants, for which he was grateful.

Chapter 37

Two Hawks also felt a barely perceptible increase in moisture in the air, along with a gradual leveling of the terrain around the river, understanding that the Colorado had begun to meander down through the very wide coastal plain bordering the great salt water.

The knowledge he held about the land around him was comforting. He let his mind drift over his travels in all of the directions around him over the many years, drift to long discussions with Dr. Sibley and even with Margaret and young Peter, and he understood that sadness in the doctor's eyes, that knowledge did not often bring happiness or even pleasure, that knowledge polished into wisdom was a stone, not a pillow, may be beautiful but was not always good, whatever that may be.

Two Hawks had a reasonable understanding of how large this earth was, how many creatures were crawling over it, knew that his own people and so many of the other tribes understood their own small worlds but knew nothing of the rising flood that would sweep them from the land, would unceasingly wash away their villages and children and every sign of their way of life. Even the Comanche in their momentary dominance and ferocity were building mud walls to hold back a rising sea. Such knowledge held no comfort and, like a polished stone whose face shown out from hard ground, was of no use.

But somewhere ahead lay if not an answer at least a reason for his being pulled so far south. He mulled this over, hand draped over the limb tiller, late afternoon of the third day on the river, slowly chewing what he realized was his last strip of boucan, the French form of jerked beef he especially relished, and rounding an oxbow meander surprised several longhorns that had come down through a soft break in the steep banks to drink.

The cows snapped their heads up out of the water like a single animal, the river water pouring from their wide snouts, their parti-colored hides not unlike a group of mustangs though a bit rustier, these slower beasts having time to oxidize in the heat and rain. But their wide-spread horns and rolling eyes dispelled any kinship to the passive bovines of cultured pastures.

A low snort from one of the heifers, her calf new and soft as a suede purse, set the animals in motion, and they spun on knotted legs and planted hooves, and drove up through the gap in the hard clay bank and vanished.

Again, Two Hawks decided to utilize another animal's access to the river as his landing, pulling the boat well up the churned bank before securing it to the base of a thick sapling out of the midst of the churned path.

After gathering his pouches and rifle once again and reaching the level ground above the river, in the falling day he caught sight of a small flock of turkeys drifting sedately through a series of clearings created by the canopies of old live oaks. Settling his gear high up in one of the trunks, he took out a coil of sinew he thought to use, perhaps to string another bow, but instead thought of a more immediate use.

Choosing an oak at some distance from his chosen bed, he picked up two fist-sized stones and gathered several hands' full of last fall's acorns preserved under the mat of dead leaves, smashing the hulls until a small pile of moist and pounded yellow meats lay at hand. He then tied a slipknot around a loop of sinew, securing the other end to a fallen limb. Propping up one end of the snare with a thin twig, he sprinkled the mast around and into the loop and made a number of fading gobbling sounds before returning to his own perch some distance away. Wild turkeys were not especially intelligent, but they were often insatiably curious, so he had a chance of success.

Wakening to the sounds of frightened gobbling and screeching, Two Hawks hastened to his trap, in part knowing full well that a coyote or fox would be drawn to the sounds of distress as well, and would be more than willing to steal the prize of his labors.

The terrified flapping of wings as he approached told him the snare had caught the turkey hen around the legs. He swiftly chased the bird to the length of the sinew, drew his knife and removed her head, gathering wings and flailing legs to his chest to aim the jetting blood away from him. Here would be meat for several days.

He decided, too, that while the pull of the spirit journey remained clear and strong as a deep-hooked fish, lines can break and fish landed too green can wreak havoc. As the warm bird stilled against his breast, he thought that he would spend the day and another night at this camp, look to his kit and vessel, watch the river, savor the crawl of old tattoos on his back.

After coiling and pouching his sinew snare for future use, Two Hawks ambled to the river, plucking the turkey as he went, removed his moccasins and waded into the shallows near his boat, gutted and washed her in the running water, watching minnows dart at the threads of blood and membrane. He tossed the liver, gizzard, and heart back onto the bank and let lungs and the rest of the innards drift away into the current, saying aloud, "Would have made fine fish bait."

Chapter 38

Not trusting the pilfering creatures that lay in wait near camp, he was sure, he tied the cleaned bird by a thong at his waist, pouched the select innards, and wandered about until he had gathered some green cedar berries, sweet young grass and, as fortune and patience would have it, a handful of wild onion and mustard. Adding a few edible mushrooms found where an oak limb had begun to disintegrate into the shade of a clearing, he circled back to his camp, approaching from another direction to surprise any potential watchers, but he was indeed alone.

A day's smoking would have rendered the meat more flavorful and less perishable, but the Caddo would not risk the visibility that it would create. He stuffed the carcass with the items he had gathered, added a healthy pinch of salt from his pouch, and stitched her closed around a skinned oak branch, the crooks in the limb helping to hold the bird in place. Heart, gizzard, and liver he would roast separately during the day as rewards for his patience. The live oak canopies held years of dry hardwood for a virtually smokeless fire.

The meat on, between forked branches, Two Hawks dragged his bateau up onto an angled drift of river sand and turned it over, inspecting the seams, as the old German had suggested to Peter. Using his knife and a smooth river stone, he gently tapped several lengths of the tarred oakum twists he carried into the seams where he had earlier noted seepage to the boat's interior.

It was the kind of labor he enjoyed, meticulous, purposeful, carried out with a focus and concentration that allowed contemplation of otherness but only enough for a single line of thought. Such tasks frequently led to solved problems or clarified destinations.

Soon the sun was at its height, and Two Hawks fixed a weak cup of tea sweetened with some of the final shavings of dark sugar from the diminished cone he had carried since Fort Jessup. The rich gizzard he chewed on added to his satisfaction.

As the day began to wear into the thin light of dusk, nudged by his earlier memory of the tips of cattails poking up from a sinkhole pond not far from the clearing where he sat, the old man thought he may as well make his repast complete. Finding the new marsh plant growth thick and tender in the rich soil of the pond's verge, he cut four or five of the cattails near the roots and, back in camp, cut several sections the length of his forearm and placed them, wet, on the coals near the edge of his fire.

Later, the light having faded to early darkness, up off the ground and his back resting comfortably once again where a large oak's limbs joined the trunk, Two Hawks relished in memory his evening meal of slow-roasted turkey breast and back meat blended with the crusty skin in the bowl-like carcass with the herbs and mushrooms. The roasted starchy interior of peeled cattails had added a perfect balance. Turkey legs, thighs, and wings wrapped and tied in fresh grass bundles to hold in the moisture would make welcome one-handed meals to chew on as he steered downriver.

Then, on the fourth day, as the leather pouches and moccasins he wore increasingly remained damp throughout the hours of the day, and he noted fewer and fewer large treetops peeking over the banks from the surrounding plain, he thought he could smell the salt of the great water. The sooty wings etched into the skin of his back fluttered as they had not in many rounds of seasons and were still. "I am coming," he thought. "Soon now I will learn."

Chapter 39

Later that day, a dry campsite was difficult to find as the marsh beyond the river's low banks seemed to press in, patiently, like the parasites of carrion, knowing that the artery would open in time and spill its precious freight.

Settling at last for a low bank of crusted earth but finding little dry wood for a fire, he had no choice but to camp early in the dark, leaning against a grey drifted stump, his sheathed knife pulled around and resting, haft up, ready to hand between his legs. He wanted no scaly guests sharing his warmth in the night.

The pre-dawn sounds of a waking world soon afforded a welcome exit from a long disturbing dream that had brought images of his long-dead wife, named after what the whites called the passenger pigeon, but she was tightly bound in a corset and full petticoated skirt, the material in the calm dark tones Margaret Dupre preferred. She had simply stared at him with tears furrowing her soiled cheeks, but with a delicate smile curling her lips.

Clutching her left hand was Peter, but smaller, the age Two Hawks' own son had been when taken by the bear. Peter, oddly dressed in the winter doeskin hunting shirt and leggings of an Osage, had looked up at the woman as he struck himself over and over in the thigh with the broken remnant of an obsidian knife, the bright fresh blood soaking through the thin leather and squeezing out between his fingers. As dreams would have it, Two Hawks could neither move nor speak, providing neither rescue nor comfort. The mute testimony had rent his spirit to exhaustion.

So it was with some gratitude that he blinked himself awake in the oily hour before dawn, reminded that no snakes had need to seek warmth down here. The humidity dripped from nearby leaves. Two Hawks hung his flaccid hunting vest on his shoulders like damp fabric and, seeing he was safely alone, ran his crooked hands over the faded symbols inked into his arms so many years ago, setting aswarm a cloud of swollen mosquitoes.

Rolling over onto hands and knees and finally standing, scanning his immediate surroundings, the old Caddo roused the squawk and beat of immense wings as a great blue heron was disturbed from his first wade, and Two Hawks gently chided himself for not spending more caution at rising.

Urinating into the slack marsh water, he slowly chewed the last gristle of a turkey leg and watched three stick-legged pink birds wade slowly in the shallow flat nearby, their long necks and heads sweeping back and forth in the growing light, occasionally lifting bills ending in spatulate strainers from the calm water.

"Today," he said aloud, speaking to the bateau as he stowed his pouches and musket. "Today the river will join the sea, and I will let you go."

The landscape continued to flatten beyond the trees that fringed the banks of the river as morning was burned away by a bright sun, and through the branches the horizon seemed alight along its length with a luminous white haze.

Two Hawks recognized the approaching coast where the breakers dashed moisture and salt into the air as they beat themselves to foam beyond dunes bearded with broom grass and thick vines.

Rounding one last bend in the widening river that had slowed as it approached the shoulder of the tide, he saw ahead open sea and steered his bobbing craft toward the western bank. Two Hawks was grateful to find low tide, an expanse of river bank laid bare on either side presenting itself for his choosing. The sounds of waves breaking in the rising land breeze brought him to steer into a shallow impression in the bank, the boat's wooden prow grinding past oysters to a soft stop in the sandy mud with a sigh.

The sound not lost on Two Hawks, the old Caddo slid off his moccasins and stepped into the warming water, tugging the boat further up onto the strand to unload but also smiling as he said aloud, "You have served me well, little bateau," liking the French word with its soft bird-like sound over the hard close of the English word "boat."

"I understand by your sound that you are tired, but while your journey has not ended, I will lighten your freight."

He carefully laid his pouches and rifle on pads of bunched grass, removed the coils of oakum that remained, tucked them tightly under the oak seat for someone else's use, and rested his hand on the weathered bow. He then sent the boat with a healthy push back out into the current that soon sent its reduced weight bobbing west and south, and he watched the craft until it became only a speck on the shining expanse of water hastening to merge with the sea.

"Go, little bateau," he repeated. "You may tumble and break on the bar, but I think you will be cast into the quieter water and pushed up onto the softer shore, perhaps to be found before sun and time shrink you to grey bones in the sand."

Two Hawks stood, adjusting his pouches and the heavy Charleville musket onto his back, and turned his steps to the expanse of sand and mud clotted with saltbush, here and there saw palms rearing their shaggy heads. His general direction was southwest, paralleling the coast, he knew; but his makeshift path between the stiff thick bushes sometimes ended in salt marsh ponds and flats, and he would circle around until finding firmer ground.

By afternoon he had reached the flat, still water that stretched to the southwest further than the eye could see but encircled to the south by a thin line of low vegetation and sand. Matagorda Bay—the tattooed talon lines on his arms stretched and seemed to pull tight deep beneath his skin like healing wounds, and he removed his moccasins, tying them to his waist with a thong.

Chapter 40

The shoreline of the bay was for the most part a soft walk of mud and thin drifted sand, broken by marle outcroppings and bands of petrified oyster shell. He made good time.

As the sun began its slide toward the western beard of stunted oaks, Two Hawks lingered at an abandoned fish camp, the ashes of several fires bordered by scorched oyster shells and the cleaned backbones of numbers of large fish, three piles of smeared temporary drying racks cast aside. One broken clay vessel blackened with sea tar spoke of Karankawa, though the condition of the ashes beaten almost flat by showers suggested that the band had moved on at least two days ago.

In the shallows along the shore, Two Hawks surprised four blue crabs working their pincers on a sizeable redfish the Karankawa may have wounded and lost. The fish's eye was still bright and clear, so he chased the crabs from their feast and dragged the ragged carcass up onto the shore.

Several pounds of reasonably fresh fish remained intact, and Two Hawks found to his surprise that the gullet still held three shrimp and a few fingerling mullet, all of which after a careful rinsing he wrapped in the fillets. Not wanting to discover that this was a regularly visited camp, he moved on and saw no other sign of habitation that day.

After roasting the redfish fillets held together in two peeled twig baskets, the shrimp and minnows steaming inside and imbuing a complex flavor to the whole, Two Hawks let his low fire, banked behind drifted sand and rush, burn low and go out. His memories of Fish Eye and his own missing finger of flesh were still keen, and he now had even less to spare, so he sat in the sand in the growing dark, his back against a sun-bleached trunk of a drifted tree, far enough up from the high-tide band of brown seagrass and Sargasso to avoid waking in water but close enough so the constant breeze out on the narrow peninsula he had selected kept most of the mosquitoes from finding him. The sandflies, however, seemed to inhabit the very air he breathed.

Morning came damp and sticky, as it often did down here. Two Hawks would need to find a supply of fresh water, and in following the shore he discovered himself pacing north until he was on once-familiar ground, the Karankawa village, or where it had been, soon coming into view.

The clearing was long abandoned, however, marked only by several smoke-stained rock rings. His encounter years earlier rushed over his consciousness in waves, but these memories were supplanted by an overbearing sense of loss, not his own but for the simple, if severe, people who had squatted around these fire rings, taking what they needed from the sea, leaving scant residue of their passing. He felt, knew, that their small and fragile numbers were being swept from the surface of this enduring earth. The fish camp had been a remnant only.

Looking again seaward, Two Hawks had a vision, of all the tears in the world, from women weeping for lost children born and unborn, of ancient Caddo watering each others' cheeks in greeting, of old men in solitary weeping for their grown sons and daughters taken before they themselves had moved on from this crust of ground, even from children large and small crying at injuries imagined and real, as though the younger years were all a practice and imitation for the grief to come. He even saw tears squeezed from the dark egg-sized eyes of injured horses, the thick tears he had once glimpsed—or imagined he had—from the down-draped head of a heavy doe after his steel-tipped shaft had dropped her buck first to his forelegs and then onto his heaving side, even the sand-crusted rheum-thick tears of a sea turtle after laboriously shoveling in the scoopings over her heap of sticky eggs on the beach before she shouldered beneath the foaming waves and was seen no more. He saw all of these tears falling, collecting somehow into unseen rivulets that flowed beneath rocks and grass and hungry roots, at last the swelling into salty streams that released their burden into the endless sea.

The screeching laugh of a black-headed gull slapped Two Hawks' vision aside, but still he lingered, wondering if that were why the broad sweep of sea to beyond the horizons so often brought sadness but unspoken comfort as well, a sea of tears it was.

He did not linger further in the haunted spot but was grateful in the knowledge that what the Spanish called the Tres Palacios River was an easy walk.

Finding the river later that day where the flow spread out into the wide bay, he crossed at low tide, going back and filling an oiled leather water bag deep in the colder flow. He once again cold camped, chewing on the last of the redfish he had dried over the diminishing coals the preceding night.

But the breeze dropped during the night, and the mosquitoes came for him. He awoke with so many punctures that he imagined himself considerably lighter in weight, the precious red fluid carried off half a drop at a time into the humid dark.

In late morning, Two Hawks squatted on the dense grey mud that fringed the shining disk of Matagorda Bay, watching two shore crabs rise out of their holes, seeming to taste as well as see the humid spring day with their eye-stalks. He remained motionless, still as the drifted button-wood nearby, as the minutes passed, and gradually the crabs crept closer, closer, until one began pinching at the thick leathery sole of his foot that was deeply cracked by rough ground and salt marsh. To preserve has moccasins, he had tied them to his waistbelt.

He smiled slowly at the pinch of the crabs, knowing how they waited, something always waited to feed as others fell. Soon, little ones, he thought, and turned at the sound of gunfire, boom, boom boom, boom, breaking the stillness of the day, and the crabs shot back into their holes as his toes gripped the broken shells in the mud and he raised his black eyes, one increasingly clouded over, a haze on his right side that had begun three months ago, before he had turned his steps to Natchitoches.

Chapter 41

Across this pocket of the bay, to the east a cloud of egrets and storks rose into the bright morning haze, but numbers fluttered back to earth, like handfuls of white flower petals between the fingers of a palsied hand. Boom boom, boom, boom, the faint percussions drifted over the impassive mud flats. The feather hunters were stuffing their bags, he knew, for fashion.

"I remember," he said aloud, a green heron cocking its head at the sound, one long leg poised to step further into the warm water, toes spread.

And he thought back through all those rounds of seasons, friends, companions, long dead or drifted to the whites, or further back into the stony wild that was beyond the monks and the mesquite, to the west or north. He remembered when he had begun to think about the sounds his father and mother sometimes made together in their conical straw dwelling, and he himself had looked at the girls, at their bodies, in a new way. They had lived much further north then, and east. But one summer they had gone down to the big salt water, and he had looked across the water there on the upper reaches of Galvez where the bright birds floated down onto the islands to the east, the low islands that stretched into the Gulf and kept the waters quiet where their people fished and gathered oysters and crabs. He had told his father he wanted to go out to the islands, paddle out there and catch some birds, for meat, he had said, but knew he wanted to make a feather bonnet for the girl on the other side of the clearing who looked at him with soft brown eyes and made him look away in embarrassment.

His father had looked hard at him, deep into the boy's eyes, and had said, "We will go and see the old man tomorrow," nodded, squeezed the boy's shoulder, and strode away.

The following morning, his father shook him awake and they walked out into the dark morning of the season before the long heat, the bushes and sawgrass dripping in the dawn, made water together near the edge of the clearing, and came back to the cold fire, filling pouches with smoked mullet and berries that hung over the coals. The stream water was cool to their throats, and they rose and followed the hard path that led south.

Just before noon, he followed his father down a side trail to the east and, leaving their pouches and knives, all but two bags made of knotted vine, they waded into the still waters in the lee of a finger of low sand. Schools of mullet jumped lazily, one darted in a curled vee beyond the reach of some prowling shark. The boy and his father began to feel forward with their feet, soon encountering the encrusted beds of oysters in the warm waist-deep water. According to the instructions of his father, they gathered four handfuls each of the fat shells long as their open hands and waded ashore. "For the old one," his father said, and the two continued their pace south.

Just past an old red oak, its trunk disfigured like the hind leg of a deer that had been broken and mended poorly after the boy had stalked and shot it with his bow in the last frozen rain, his father's stick-straight back and tireless stride shifted west, seemingly into the midst of the dense palmettos and scrub oaks. At first, the boy had difficulty picking out the trail, so overgrown it was, but he soon began to notice up-croppings of limestone and harder rock among the fallen branches, rock that was polished smooth by the soles of passing feet, and the boy felt a brush of fear, as when last spring a panther's print in the fresh mud had filled with water as he watched.

His father pushed on, rapidly, driven in a way the boy was not accustomed to, until after the trail circled around two hackberry trees draped in wild grapes and then widened to a clearing painted suddenly crimson and gold as the sun plunged down.

In the dying light, at the clearing's edge rose a mound of whitened oyster shell, tall as a man, and near the center of the grass-tufted clearing, next to a ring of smooth and tight-fitting fire stones sat the old one.

After the sparks caught the moss tinder and sent tiny tongues of flame up into the twigs, catching twisted grey branches alright, the old man accepted the bags of oysters with a nod and carefully laid out the swollen shells in a row. He then brought a curious copper tool like a sharpened thumb out of a beaded pouch and began to pry open the shells, each with a hollow pop that made the boy's mouth run with saliva.

As the man worked, the boy shyly stole glances at this old one they had traveled to see, but the man did not look like the old ones he had seen among his people, and this was certainly not a white old one, either. Chapetyl, his father had called him, was the color of oiled cedar, dark reddish brown, with thick grey strands of hair falling only below his ear under a curious collection of bright red and green and yellow feathers bound to his head in a manner the boy had never seen. Most odd was the man's face—round jaw, receding chin, jutting lips, and thick hooked nose, like a stone hatchet, the man's face was, the eyes glittering black and shining, like the tiny arrow points he had seen from the south.

They ate, almost drank, the sweet oyster meats in the cooling dark around a yellow ring of flickering light, ate in silence, each buried in his own thoughts, the boy noticing as the flames began to crackle and blink green and red and blue, wondering if the salt caused that, then his father broke the night.

"The boy wants to go to the islands, after the birds."

Chapter 42

"Humph," the old man had grunted, looking like one of the sad giant turtles that dragged themselves sometimes up onto the sand. He seemed to become one of these wrinkled creatures, opening his beak and beginning: "The storm god gathers the feathers of those birds for his cloak. You see them on some days sweeping the highest part of the sky, out of reach."

"There was a season long ago when the large birds lived here with us on the shore and we shared the fish and the crabs and the storm god came sometimes to gather his feathers but we knew him. But then came a people who killed, a people who killed people and birds and animals with little cause, who took birds with arrows and crept up onto the birds' nests in the dark and grabbed the birds by their long legs and killed and ate the tiny young birds until the birds cried out, screamed out loud and long for the storm god to help them."

"Far to the south, in the southern sea where the water is warm as blood, the sleeping storm god raised his heavy eyes and heard the screams and cries of his beloved birds, and he arose and called to his great black thunder bird that carried him over the water, his bird Hurakan, and the storm god grew sad and then angry as he listened, so that he grew darker and swelled and lightning bolts broke from his brow and torrents of tears poured from his eyes ..."

The boy had been staring into the colors of the crackling fire but looked up at the old man, whose words were pounding out as steadily as the beating of a drum but his lips no longer moved and his eyes stared straight ahead into the night.

"And Hurakan rose and spread his black wings and began to beat them, the powerful feathers rending the sky, the air pushing the water into sharp peaks broken with white foam, and the storm god rode north on Hurakan, slowly, feeling the powerful muscles of his carrier beneath him, driven by the cries of the herons and storks, the egrets and terns that echoed across to expanse of the Gulf."

Again the boy raised his eyes and dimly saw the old man across the fire, his hard face shining, lips pressed together in anger, but the darkness throbbed with his voice, held the boy like hands pressing his shoulders down, his bare flanks feeling the broken shell and coarse sand imprinting his skin. His father sat motionless next to him, eyes closed, palms open on his knees, mouth hung loose at rest.

"The people who lived with the birds felt the sky hold its breath, saw the pelicans staying close in and low and looked out over the still water turning flat and grey. Far to the south at the edge of sight they saw the darkness spreading across the rim of earth, sweeping forward. As the day drew to a close they saw the wings of Hurakan black and tattered tearing across the sky and felt the anger of the storm god and were afraid."

"All that night and into the following day the storm god held Hurakan hovering, panting, beating its terrible wings upon them and the storm god cried for his birds. The huge wings of Hurakan pushed and swept the waters of the Gulf up onto the land, far back into the land, until the people climbed high into the trees. Many of the new people did not know Hurakan, did not understand the water, and were drowned or were swept hard against the trees until their bodies broke, found later like old blankets draped over limbs ..."

"On the afternoon of the second day, the storm god grew tired of his anger and turned his great bird and bid it to beat its wings back into the Gulf. As Hurakan withdrew, beating and pulling his great black wings, the waters fell, but as they fell Hurakan gathered and pushed back the land into the Gulf with his thick wings and clawing feet until all along the shore but separated from the land by shallow water Hurakan built up a row of islands from the mud and sand he had dragged back, making a home for the birds of the storm god."

"As the last long pinions of Hurakan's plumes receded that afternoon, the storm god opened his colored cloak and let beams of sunlight burn down onto the new islands off the shore to show the birds the way, and they came and began to pace and strut and probe about in the mud and sand as the sun came out brilliant and sparkled on the glittering sea. The islands smoked and steamed in the sun like loaves of browned maize. The storks looked one to another as others wheeled down and wagged their thick heads, egrets strutted in the drying pools and with the herons speared frantic fish and slid them down long throats, ruffling their plumes contentedly. Far overhead the sandhill cranes circled and called to their far away homes. Terns chattered and probed the fresh sand with their sensitive beaks, and all the flocks knew the islands were their home, knew the storm god had heard their cries."

As the last droning fall of Chapetyl's voice was absorbed into the night, the boy looked up over the red and grey broken coals from the fire and saw the old man nod forward onto his chest, his necklace strands of pink and yellow shells glowing dully in the gloom. An immense fatigue swept over the boy, and his arms wrapped his knees, he asleep before his forehead rested.

The dawn light had wakened the boy, and he unfolded awkwardly, feeling the slick damp of the salt-coast air clinging like grease to his limbs, his hair wet to the touch. The fire was cold, and squatting on his hams next to the boy sat his father, impassive, almost amused.

"Where is the old man?" the boy asked.

"He has gone away."

"But where? Did you see him go?"

His father stared hard at him, turned down the corners of his hard mouth in what he felt a smile, and said, "You know."

The boy had known, and the understanding had made him glad that he soon would be a boy no more, and sad as the weight of knowledge sometimes settles on one's shoulders like a heavy burden, a bag of stones.

Two Hawks heard again, far off, the boom of the feather hunters' guns, but thought instead they were the distant thunder of another storm and he smiled, as his father had, turning down the corners of his mouth. His did not feel the pinch of the crabs this time, did not feel the tiny claws pry open the cracks on his toes, did not see the bright red beads of blood as they tasted. He was instead mesmerized by the little girl no older than six rounds of seasons in a soiled and torn blue gingham dress, her feet bare and bloody, who wandered toward where he stood, but her head hung down so she saw nothing more than a few paces in front of her feet. She held her head tightly down, he then saw, to keep the blood from running out of the long gash where her throat had been cut.

He had come for this, he knew, and the wings on his back stirred. The girl, in some way herself a sign of purpose, of endurance, roused Two Hawks from his slide and, feeling suddenly the prying claws of the crabs, he stepped back, sending them shooting sideways toward their holes, and felt as though he had stepped back from the crumbling verge of a fathomless abyss.

His abrupt movement at the edge of the girl's peripheral vision caused her to stop in her tracks. She remained motionless, head down, as the old Caddo stepped in front of her trajectory and squatted on his heels scarce an arm's length in front of her so that she might appraise his intrusion, though her surprise at what he knew must be a terrifying sight was very brief, her sad pale eyes seeming so aged and resigned to the horrors of this world that death at the hands of this ancient tattooed Indian might even be a welcome end.

Two Hawks was deeply dismayed at the thoughts he read in the spirit of one so young to the journey and spoke deep and low: "Little sister, no harm will come to you here. You have died enough for one day. Let us sit and take a look at your neck—no, do not fear—if the cut would kill you it would have done so before now ..."

She knelt in the sand and sat to the side, her ragged skirts folded under her legs, though her somnambulant movements indicated that she had resigned herself to whatever new suffering might be at hand. He moved her long matted hair behind her ears, leaned over and raised her trembling chin, seeing bright new blood beneath the old but saw that the cut, though almost from ear to ear, was not so deep as to sever the powerful pumping tubes that would empty her small frame.

"Listen to me, child," he said, gathering her thin bloodstained fingers into his creased old hands. "I will make you better, believe me, and we will go to your home—" but he stopped at seeing tears fill her eyes anew, gathering that what she had called home may only hold more death now. "I will find people for you, your kind of people, but we must first repair your neck."

Something in the old man's tone and hands bade the girl believe him, and she gave an almost imperceptible nod.

"We will build a fire for water and tea and then wash your cut in the sea—it will sting," he said, "and then I will sew you back together as neat and pretty as any doll you ever saw," which caused her to imagine that and reward him with the faintest of smiles.

He rose, untied the pouches at his waist, and thanked Dr. Sibley for pressing the tiny curved needle and coil of catgut upon him so many days ago in Natchitoches. His wings seemed to flutter and settle.

www.ingramcontent.com/pod-product-compliance
Lightning Source LLC
Chambersburg PA
CBHW030130260626
47156CB00008B/2875

9 781942 956587